Aimee's Ghost

In Loving Memory of My Grandfather
Alfred Martin Wilson

Cover and book design by
Mary Fischer of Fischer Studio Works Inc.

Present Day ~ Port Townsend

A brisk spring breeze rolled across Aimee, tossing her long auburn hair in-front of her face and raising goose bumps on her arms. Opening the vehicle's back door she removed her cardigan and put it on. While she stood there next to the rental car, she found it difficult to contain her excitement as she mentally envisioned how grand the Stuart Estate looked during its' prime. The massive Victorian, which was built in the Second Empire style with a mansard roof, stood majestically on the bluff overlooking Port Townsend and Admiralty Bay.

From below, at town level, the mansion must have appeared as an imposing God keeping watch over everything it surveyed. The property was flanked on three sides by groves of indigenous trees and a variety of fruit orchards and gardens, keeping it secluded from the rest of the world.

Aimee imagined a horse-drawn carriage delivering prominent guests to the mansion along the same road she had just traveled. They would have viewed the Bay along their left-side as the carriage emerged from the trees and traveled past vast orchards and gardens to their right. Approaching the mansion the carriage would have slowed, allowing the passengers a chance to breathe in the multitude of fragrances from the extensive flower gardens, as it followed the road to the right and pulled onto the heavily graveled circular drive before stopping in front of the main steps and door.

Today the drive is still visible, but a secondary dirt road continues on straight, past the turn for nearly 200 feet, then veers to the right and runs in front of the house until it abruptly ends at the grove of trees. Both the road and the circular drive are divided by an ornate iron fence and the interior of the drive holds the last remaining memories of a stone structure and what possibly was a manicured garden.

Retrieving the property advertisement from her bag Aimee compared it to the actual house. The ad showed one slightly blurry, side-angle view of the front which cleverly hid the jungle that was once a vast yard and gardens. Clearly the agent did not want potential buyers seeing the enormity of the refurbishment project before they actually arrived at the location. This way, potential buyers would create their own mental images and fall in love with the property in their head. Once they arrived, hopefully they would be so attached to their mental image that they would not actually see what was before them. Aimee chuckled to herself because the ploy worked! She had mentally fallen in love with the house.

Vines grew heavily along the porch, giving the impression they were pulling the roof line down to the railings. Tree branches intertwined into neighboring trees and what once were manicured shrubs were now enormous in size and grotesquely shaped. The new grass that was attempting to grow was immediately lost under a thick growth of weeds that seemed to choke its spirit for life as soon as it sprouted. Aimee realized she had definitely worn the wrong shoes to walk around the outside of this house.

Aimee wondered why the Realtor never mentioned the amazing view or the tremendous possibilities the place held. She simply told her the house was built in 1856 and was extremely run-down. Actually, the more she thought about her conversations with the Realtor, the more it seemed the Realtor was trying to keep her from looking at the property.

The sound of a car door shutting brought Aimee out of her thoughts. Turning her view from the house back towards the Bay, she realized the Realtor had arrived and was parked on the dirt road. Shutting her car door, Aimee went to meet the agent.

"Hi, I'm Kate and you must be Aimee," the Realtor stated as she extended her arm and hand but didn't move more than a few inches from her car. "How was the drive?"

"Oh the drive was fine; quicker than I thought it would be. I've been here a while so it gave me a chance to enjoy this lovely view," Aimee replied.

"You must have been looking at Admiralty Bay because looking this direction," she said turning towards the house, "is tragic!"

"I don't know if I'd go that far, but I do agree it needs a lot of work."

"Why hasn't anyone bought and restored the property? With this fantastic view they could have flipped it and made a fortune," Aimee commented.

"Actually, the original owners required it stay in the Stuart family and prohibited their descendants from selling the house and the current five-acres of land it now sits on. Only one problem, there hasn't been a relative who desired to live here since the late 1890's.

Basically they used it as a rental but kept finding the tenants left abruptly after a few weeks. It's been empty since the mid 1970's."

"Wow, I bet the upkeep was a nightmare for a renter to manage."

"Something like that," Kate replied.

"So if the family can't sell it, why is it on the market now?"

"The last known Stuart descendant died and his Estate is selling it to pay off the debts."

Aimee watched Kate as they stood by her car and talked. Periodically Kate would glance towards the house, but never actually focused her gaze on it. She kept Aimee's attention on the Bay views, as if waiting for something or expecting something to happen and not wanting Aimee to witness it.

"Will you show me the inside?" Aimee inquired. "Then we can walk the grounds. Well the areas that aren't impassable by years of neglect," she said lifting up her foot to show why walking would be difficult. "Note to one's self: Stilettos are not appropriate footwear for tracking through dense jungle," she said with a laugh.

"Sure, anytime you're ready," Kate said, extending her arm towards the circular drive.
At that moment Kate's cell rang, "Go on ahead dear, the doors not locked. I need to take this call."

"Not a problem," Aimee replied.

Aimee actually preferred viewing the house alone; she always felt pressured with a Realtor looking over her shoulder. This way she could take her time and really get a feel for the place.

As Aimee opened the front door and stepped inside, her heart jumped with excitement. She found herself standing in a very large foyer that was open to the second floor. The beauty of the house took her breath away. True, it needed a lot of work, but Aimee immediately saw beyond that.

To her left was a set of sliding pocket doors that opened onto a living room with a large bay window overlooking the water and on the opposite wall from the living room door was a beautiful stone fireplace. On the wall opposite the bay window there was a single door that led into a study which had a large window on the left wall and a smaller fireplace.

Back in the foyer, across from the living room Aimee viewed another set of sliding pocket doors that opened onto a formal dining room with an identical bay window as the living room and on the opposite wall rom the window was another beautiful fireplace which was flanked with built-in china cupboards that were enclosed with leaded glass doors.

A small colorful stream of light, midway up the staircase, forced Aimee to tilt her head backwards and look up to see where the light was coming from. Just above the main entrance, at the second floor level was a large double window and centered on that window was a massive crystal chandelier. Her first thought was to step out from underneath it, wondering how something that large had stayed in place for so long with little to no maintenance.

On the first floor Aimee also discovered a laundry area, two bathrooms, a large kitchen with eating area, a bedroom and two screened-in porches off the back of the house.

Climbing up the servant stairs located off the laundry room, Aimee arrived on the main second floor landing. This floor provided four additional bedrooms and two full baths. Going back to the servant stairs she climbed to the third floor where the servants would have resided. Over the years it appeared that whatever structures had been in place were gone and all that remained was a dark, musty and very dirty space. This was definitely not a place she wanted to investigate.

Heading back down to the master suite Aimee knew this was her dream house. She could imagine herself sitting in front of this very window in her new master suite, watching the activity on the Bay and witnessing the spectacular storms as they rolled in.

Looking down to the road she could see Kate standing next to her car, arms crossed, just staring at the house. Aimee tapped on the window and motioned for her to come inside, but Kate acted as if she did not see her.

Aimee turned away from the window and hurried down the stairs and out the front door.

"Kate!" she yelled.

"Oh my God, what happened!?" she yelled taking a step backwards.

Kate's reaction startled Aimee and she paused halfway down the drive.

"Well nothing, I'm just excited about the house and wanted to see if you had a contract with you."

"Oh," she said, acting a bit more relaxed.

"Why did you think something happened?" Aimee asked.

"Sorry, it was nothing. You just surprised me when you ran out of the house like that. I was lost in thought… and yes, I do have a contract, but there are a few things I need to tell you about the house before you make an offer."

"Things, like what?" Aimee asked.

"Let's go into town and get a coffee. We can relax and talk there," Kate said as she opened her car door and stepped inside the vehicle.

Aimee realized Kate was not going to talk here. "Okay, I'll follow you into town."

In her excitement, Aimee did not notice the front door, which she had left open, slowly close behind her. Kate on the other hand witnessed the massive door closing and knew exactly what it meant.

As Aimee pulled into the parking lot of the Morning Fuel coffee house she was determined to get to the bottom of the matter. If Kate did not want to work with her for some personal reason, fine, give the sale to another agent. Or if Kate had another buyer and was trying to discourage the sale in an attempt to get multiple offers going and start a bidding war, then she wanted to know now. Simply being rude and non-helpful was not going to chase her away.

"Okay," Aimee said as she sat down at the table across from Kate. "What is going on with the house and why are you so opposed to me purchasing it?"

Aimee couldn't believe she'd been so direct with Kate, as she emptied the sugar packet into her cup of coffee. Usually she avoided conflict at all cost, but at this moment she knew she was willing to fight for this house.

"I'm sorry if I've given you the wrong impression," Kate said as she starred at the cream swirling around in her coffee; slowly looking up at Aimee, 'it's just that you're young and single and I'm concerned for you."

"Concerned about what? I've been on my own for years, I have a great home office job and finances for the house purchase and restoration are not an issue. What are you concerned about?"

Kate could not keep her gaze directed toward Aimee, which made Aimee think she was hiding something.

"Really dear, it's just that the house is massive and has been abandoned for so long that I fear it is a huge money pit."

"Is that all?" Aimee asked, a little angry. "Last year I was left in a coma for nearly two months, after being hit by a drunk driver. The settlement was substantial and I decided life is too short to dream about the future so I am buying the Stuart home so I can restore it and live in my dream house now."

Kate reached across the table, placing her hand on top of Aimee's. "I am so sorry; how terrible." Keeping her gaze on Aimee's hand Kate blurted out, "Honey, the house is haunted. There - I said it."

Aimee burst out laughing, but stopped quickly when she looked at Kate's face and realized she was not trying to be funny. Kate was now sitting sternly in her chair with her arms crossed.

"You're serious aren't you?" Aimee said.

"Yes, I am. Ever since the three Stuart sisters died mysteriously in that house no one has been able to live there. Many have tried, but they all leave and they all have the same stories - about objects moving, frightening sounds and the feeling that someone or something is watching them."

"Honestly Kate? I didn't feel anything strange when I was in there. I actually felt excitement about the possibilities. I'm not saying I don't believe in ghosts, but I really don't think the place is haunted. Even if it is, I guess we'll just have to get used to each other."

"You mean you still want to buy the place?" Kate asked, as she relaxed and reached for her coffee.

"Yes, I do. I really want to own that house!" she said with such enthusiasm that Kate knew she would never be able to persuade her otherwise. Kate also decided there was no reason to tell her the rest of the story and put unnecessary thoughts in her head.

"Kate, would you mind if I leave now and go back up to the house to take a few pictures while you draw up the contract? It'll be dark soon and I want some pictures to look at this evening."

"You want to go up there by yourself!?" Kate gasped.

"Well, I do plan to live there by myself, day and night, so I don't see a problem going there alone now," she said with a chuckle.

"Yes of course. I've lived here my whole life and obviously got caught up in the stories.   Just stop by my office when you are done and you can sign the documents. I'll fax them off to the estate attorney and we should hear back in a few days."

"Perfect, I'll be back shortly," Aimee said as she jumped up from her chair and grabbed her bag from the floor.

****

The sound of a motor vehicle roused Martin from the stillness of his solitary eternity. He had been alone for such a long time the thought of anyone entering the house was exhilarating; even if he must chase them away in the end. He could barely see the person sitting in the car through the years of grime that covered the nursery window and he impatiently waited for him or her to emerge.

So many people, both men and women, had arrived at the mansion over the years, and he instantly knew he did not like them, nor did he want them to reside within the property. Martin recalled the last woman who attempted to live in Stuart Mansion; she wore white boots that went up to her knees and crazy colored short dresses. She and a man arrived in a motor vehicle that was painted with flowers and wild colors. Their vehicle was oblong in shape and appeared much smaller than it really was. When the door on the side finally slid open, half-a-dozen people spilled out, like puss from an infected wound. He would never let a man stay even one night, but the woman gave him pause, and he allowed her to remain long enough to determine if she was the "one."

The man and woman were loud and so were the friends who stayed with them. Their music screamed through the walls, rattling the windows and chandeliers; the liquor flowed day and night.

Martin made life miserable for them with infestations of flies, foul smells and, in the end, physical attacks upon the man, but they just kept drinking and smoking. Then one day a lawman arrived from town. Martin watched in amusement as the man tried to intimidate the visitor with yelling and wild hand gestures but once the lawman put his hand on his weapon, the man went lifeless like a child's toy. That night they left and never returned. Even though he did not like them, there were times he missed them. It was lonely being alone.

Martin feared that in the early days he had scared away the wrong person; that his only chance for happiness was forever lost. In his initial confusion and anger over being a ghost and finding himself trapped in the Stuart Mansion, he terrorized everyone who entered the house just because he could. All that changed when he overheard two people in the front parlor talking about something they had heard in town. There was a message pinned to every single wall in the house. Each message read the same: *Guard the children's memories -- Wait for her love to free you.* No one understood the reason for the message but it struck a chord in Martin's memory and he stopped chasing people away before he had a chance to learn a little about them, but he never really understood the message.

A movement on the ground below brought Martin back to this moment. He realized there was a woman walking around, but staying close to the vehicle. She had long, flowing auburn hair and was wearing a pretty dress that swirled around her legs when she walked. He thought she looked like a hummingbird, flitting back and forth with excitement. Rushing downstairs to the master bedroom window, Martin hoped he could get a better look at her, but by the time he reached the window she had turned her back to him as she gazed out to the Bay. Martin desperately wanted her to turn back towards the house so he could study her face. He considered doing something, anything to get her attention but did not want to frighten her away. Not yet at least; not until he was sure she wasn't the one.

Martin's attention was lost on the woman and he did not hear or see the other motor vehicle arrive. Once the woman headed towards the dirt road he spotted the vehicle. The driver was the woman that brought all the wrong people to the house; he did not like her because she was loud and never stopped talking. He watched the two as they talked and wondered what they were looking at when they both looked down at the ground and the pretty woman laughed. Martin was confused on how to react when they both headed towards the mansion: Should he isolate the woman he did not like and frighten her, or leave them alone so he didn't frighten the pretty one away? To his relief the other woman was not moving forward, but had stopped walking. He was pleased that only the pretty woman was entering the house.

****

Aimee woke the following morning, to her surprise, with a call from Kate informing her that the offer had been accepted as is, and that she could close on the property within two weeks.

Not wanting to waste any time, she immediately began

searching the web for contractors to start the renovation; however, to her surprise, she could not convince anyone in the local area to take on the project. They all said they were too busy, but Aimee believed it was due to the childish ghost stories. Eventually she found a crew in Bremerton that was eager to work on a charming, but dilapidated Second Empire Victorian. Apparently, ghost stories are only frightening in their home towns of origin.

Aimee expected to stand out in a small town as the new kid on the block, but she didn't expect all the whispers and reactions she received from people when they found out she was the new owner of Stuart Mansion. Everyone wanted to know if she was okay, was anything happening and how long did she plan to 'stick it out.' Each time she just smiled and said she loved the town and planned to be part of the community for a very long time.

Aimee's goal was to save as much as possible from the original house and use reproduction or actual restored pieces to make up the difference. During the weeks that passed between the acceptance of her purchase offer and the first day the contractors were scheduled to view the property, she kept herself busy taking room measurements and shopping for historic paint and reproduction cupboards, molding and light fixtures.

The day to meet the restoration company finally arrived and Aimee woke to black skies and a steady downpour of rain. By the time she reached Stuart Mansion the sun began to shine and she decided that was a good omen.

Once inside the house she did something many would

consider foolish, but she thought, why not, it never hurts to have good karma around you. And just in case there was a ghost, she wanted it to know she was not afraid. As she walked through each room she stated, "I am the new owner and we will live here in peace." By the time she finished the last room downstairs she thought she could hear a banging. Her heart began to race as she stood frozen; trying to listen and trying not to panic. What if Kate was right and the house really was haunted and not with a friendly ghost, but one that was evil and intended to hurt her? She had seen enough horror movies to know what the demonic possibilities were! As the banging grew louder and louder her fear took over and she ran from the back room towards the foyer, where she quickly realized, with great relief, someone was pounding on the front door.

Fredrickson Restoration specialized in old Victorians and the six-member crew did not seem daunted by the task at hand, in fact they seemed excited. Aimee pointed out what her thoughts were for each room and they agreed it was a good plan; however, they would need to have the plumbing, electrical, and duct work all redone first before any restoration work could begin. By the end of the day the crew had set up several generators to run power for their equipment. They also brought in a storage pod filled with tools and another for them to use as a staging area during bad weather, which on the Olympic Peninsula was standard this time of year.

Aimee felt like a little girl on Christmas Eve knowing that tomorrow morning her dream house was going to begin its makeover. As she got in her car and headed into town she couldn't help but feel she had found her place and now finally, could see a bright future for herself at Stuart Mansion.

Winter 1863 ~ East Coast

His leg was on fire from the lead ball that pierced his upper leg and the searing pain that raced through his limb and stomach was more than he could handle, but the cold wet mud was almost comforting as Corporal Martin Stuart laid face down in it; unable to move. His thoughts seemed oddly clear and precise at that very moment; the sounds above him weren't simply sounds of battle, but the repeated shots fired by Springfield Muskets and Harpers Ferry Rifles. He could see both his friends and enemies fall all around him and hear their individual screams as artillery ripped their bodies apart. It was during that moment he feared the end was at hand and he was about to fail his parents.

Martin's parents longed for a new life in Washington, but when the War broke out they knew that it was nothing more than a dream and their current reality was grim and full of sorrow. Fitzpatrick and Catherine Stuart had three boys fighting for both the North and South and their only daughter had died from a fever the year prior. Their dream was simple now: to see their boys returned home, able to marry and have children of their own. For Martin, the ability to fulfill his parents' wish was all that kept him strong those last few hours of that brutal battle, laying there motionless in the mud.

"Martin, I knew I'd find you resting instead of fighting," a familiar voice said in a near whisper.

"Henry, is that you?" Martin replied.

"Well, who else would be crawling through this battlefield in the mud looking for your lazy ass," he said as he placed his hand on Martin's shoulder. "How bad you hurt?"

"I got hit in my left leg. I can't feel it anymore."

"Well, that's probably good because I need to drag you out of here and you need to help by pushing with your good leg. If I leave you here until the fighting is over you will be dead."

"Do what must be done Henry" Martin said, "besides if I'm dead who will you follow out West, when all of this is over?"

Martin and Henry Baker were childhood friends. At times Martin felt closer to Henry then he did his own brothers. Both men had agreed at the onset of the War, that God willing they survive, they would head out West and make their fortunes in the new frontier. Fortune or not, all they wanted at this point was the chance to go West. The War was diminishing their dreams bit by bit each day.

By the end of the War, neither Martin nor Henry had any family left in Boston to return to. Martin went to his father's solicitor and collected what had been left for him and then he and Henry Baker agreed to travel to Washington where Martin had relatives; an Uncle and three female cousins. Although he had never met them, he was sure they would provide them a place to stay while they found work and got on their feet.

As they journeyed to their new lives, they debated over what trade to settle on. Henry wanted to work aboard a fishing boat and travel the world, while Martin wanted to own a tract of land where he could plant an orchard and earn a living from the produce grown there. Although they had different visions of the future, they both held one common goal: to put the horrors of the war behind them and live in peace.

Martin Stuart

Spring 1870 ~ Port Townsend, WA

The Windspur had been in port for a week, providing a well-deserved distraction for what was left of her crew, stocking up on necessities and trying in vain to hire additional deck hands. With the provision stowed safely in the hull, Captain Kline was not overly concerned about the shortage of willing volunteers. He believed if the government could conscript men to fight in a war, then he could do the same to acquire a crew. Come morning he would set sail with a full crew, both willing and unwilling.

Martin and Henry arrived in Port Townsend just as dusk began to fall. They decided the quickest way to find Martin's relatives would be at the local saloon where they could grab a meal and a bottle of whiskey. They were right. The bartender knew the Stuart family and sketched a very crude map to the Stuart Mansion.

Feeling relieved that their journey was now at its end, Martin and Henry did buy that bottle of whiskey and headed back to their table to celebrate. In their enthusiasm they failed to see the two men sitting in the back corner, drinking and smoking cigars, watching them closely. When the two soldiers left the saloon and headed down the street towards the stairs that lead from the dock level to the upper town, they did not notice they were being followed, not just by the two men from the saloon but also by three additional men that had been waiting in the shadows outside.

"We better get going," Martin said, "by the look of the sky, we are not going to have the moon as light for much longer."

Tucking the map in his jacket pocket, Martin grabbed the side rails of the ladder to begin his climb to the upper street. Just as his foot touched the first step he felt a strong grip on his right arm that pulled him backwards with great force. Falling hard onto the gravely street, Martin turned his head and strained his eyes in the darkness to look for his companion. Martin's ears heard Henry before his eyes could locate him.

Henry was flat on his back while two men beat him with their fists and kicked him with their feet. Once he stopped fighting back, one man pulled a bag from his pocket and began placing it over Henrys' head.

Martin felt a large rock near his hand. Grasping it tightly, he jumped up and ran towards Henry and his attackers. Slamming the rock into the side of a man's head he hoped it would give Henry a fighting chance against just one attacker instead of two. Just as Martin's arm completed the motion of the swing he felt a sharp pain in his stomach and then that piercing pain repeated itself several times. Martin grabbed his stomach and crumpled to the ground in a heap. He could hear one man yelling at the others to get their new volunteer on board and to leave the other because he was worthless now.

Martin was unaware of how long he had been lying there. His head was spinning and the pain in his stomach was crippling. Had he survived a long and brutal war only to die alone on a street? His mind was reeling with pain and anger when he remembered the map in his pocket. Perhaps he could get help from his relatives? Perhaps they would be able to offer him shelter and care; perhaps, but only if he could find the strength to climb the stairs and follow the map to their home.

Mustering up all the strength he had left in his dying body, Martin began the climb upward. Each step sent a piercing pain through his body and blasted his head; he could feel his blood flowing from the wounds but he was determined to reach the top. After what seemed like an eternity, Martin emerged on the upper street where he laid, trying to regain enough strength to continue the journey. Unsure how long he would stay conscious, he knew that he didn't have time to rest too long.

Pulling the map from his pocket he tried to memorize the directions so he would have something to focus his thoughts on instead of his own slow death. Straight for two streets, left and straight again for two more streets, then left on Stuart Lane, follow it to the end and hopefully there will be help. Martin repeated the directions over and over as he took every step, leaving a trail of blood as he went.

Before he made it to the first turn the skies let loose and a sheet of rain beat down on him, making his progress slower while the muddy earth attempted to pull him in just as it tried to do that night in the War when he was shot. Martin's spirit sank even lower as he realized Henry had crawled through the fighting to save him, yet he was unable to save Henry when he needed rescuing. Time seemed to stand still. Dogs along the journey barked at him, nipped at his ankles but they eventually gave up because of the rain. Finally

Martin reached Stuart Lane but he could not see a house, just a long lonely road. As he made the final right turn down the road he noticed two deer laying under a large tree, staying as dry as they possibly could while being sheltered from the relentless rain. The sky was dark, Martin's gait was almost at a crawl, and he had no idea how much further he needed to go.

Like an angel showing him the way, a light glowed dimly in the distance and he focused his mind on that hope. With each piercing step the light grew slightly brighter and then he realized it was a lantern in a window guiding him, or so his mind believed.

The Stuart sisters, Eliza, Jane and Clair, were up late preparing for next Friday. They had gathered a lot of ingredients and there were many concoctions to prepare for the sacred full moon event where they would continue to atone for their mothers' wrong doings. What they hadn't planned for was the visitor that was steadily moving towards their glowing lantern. As they chattered amongst themselves and shuffled containers around in the kitchen, Martin pulled himself up the last few steps and onto their front porch. With his last bit of strength he pounded on their front door and then fell with a thud to the porch were he lay, silent.

Clair was lost in her own thoughts and Eliza was the first to realize there was a noise coming from the front porch.

"Jane, did you hear that? Sounded like a boom out front," Eliza stated.

"It was probably the storm," she replied.

"No, I think something is out front. Grab the lantern; we

need to check it out."

The sisters quietly walked through the house to the front
door. Jane held the lantern while Eliza slowly opened the door.

"Oh, my Dear, there's someone lying on the porch. Clair,
come help me! Set the lantern on the table, Jane, and then we
can drag him inside the house."

Eliza rolled the body over and realized it was a young
man. "Each of you take an arm and pull, I'll grab his boots, if I can
get a grip on them through all of this mud."

As Jane and Clair began pulling on his arms to drag him over
the threshold and into the foyer, he released a very sorrowful
moan. They all stopped in their tracks and looked down at him. It
was then they realized he was bleeding from his stomach.

"Hurry Sisters, let's get him inside and into the guest room,"
Eliza said. "His clothing looks as though he has lost a tremendous
amount of blood." It took all of the strength that the three sisters
could muster to drag Martin into the guest room and pull him up
onto the bed.

"Let's get these soaked clothes off of him. Clair, get some
clean rags and the ointment. We can work on a better salve later,"
Eliza said.

While Clair gathered the items from the kitchen and pantry,
Jane and Eliza made Martin as comfortable as possible.

"I'll start a fire in the hearth to warm the room," Jane said as
Clair returned to the guest room. Clair and Eliza cleaned up the
blood and attempted to close the wounds to the best of their

abilities. They wrapped Martin's stomach with gauze, covered in their special healing ointment.

"We will take turns watching over him during the night. Jane, you and Clair go back and finish what we were working on prior to his arrival. I will sit with him for now," Eliza said.

"Shall I bring you a cup of tea?" Jane asked.

"That would be lovely, thank you Dear."

As Eliza sat with the young man she wondered what he could have done to cause such evil to befall him. She knew that they couldn't get a doctor until morning and quietly prayed that he would survive the night. The hours passed slowly. Eliza had nodded off, but woke when she heard him mumbling. "Sisters, hurry, he's starting to wake."

As the sisters stood around his bed, Martin woke for a few moments.

"You're safe now," Jane said as she patted his forehead with a damp cloth.

"Can you tell us your name?" Clair asked.

"I'm Martin Stuart, your cousin. We…," and then his eyes shut and he was unconscious again.

"Did he say our cousin?" Eliza asked. He must be one of Uncle Fitzpatrick's boys. Father spoke of them periodically."

The sisters traded off throughout the night, watching over their patient. It had been a long time since they had anyone sick in the house to care for.

Present Day ~ Port Townsend

The restoration crew was waiting on the porch when Aimee arrived; she chuckled to herself and wondered if they were more excited about this project then she was.

"How about I get a duplicate key made for you, that way you can come and go as you need," she said as she unlocked the front door. "I work from home office so I will be here most days, but cannot guarantee when."

"That would be great, Miss Morgan," the foreman and owner Paul Frederickson said. "We never know how long the drive will take and we could be here 30-minutes before you on some days."

"Please call me Aimee, and I'll get a key to you before you leave this afternoon," she said as she opened the door and stepped into the grand foyer.

"Are you starting on the kitchen first?" she asked, secretly hoping they would take it as a hint.

"Sure, if that is what you want, but remember we will also be doing all the electrical, plumbing and duct work in conjunction with doing specific rooms in the order you want," Paul said.

"That works for me. I am going to wander from room to room today, saving things I think are important or just plain interesting. So holler if you need me for anything," Aimee said as she set the stack of flattened boxes down on the floor near the foot of the stairs.

"What do you plan to do with the furniture and decorations?" Paul asked. "We will need the house empty before we can begin."

"I contacted the local thrift store and they will send a truck out this afternoon to collect all the furniture and items that have been left in the house over the years. I am keeping a few pieces of furniture and the massive grandfather clock in the foyer. A gentleman from Seattle will send a truck tomorrow to pick those items up and take them back to his workshop to restore them for me."

Aimee liked the fact that so many items had been abandoned within the house over the years. It was an added bonus to purchasing the property and gave her the opportunity to study books and possibly journals from the previous owners. In a way she felt it gave her a chance to be part of the history and connect with the house.

Taking two boxes, she headed into the pantry and began gathering the old jars and dishes that were left behind. Many items were beyond salvaging and those ended their long journey in the big dumpster that was delivered for demolition debris.

While working in the kitchen, to everyone's surprise, the crew discovered a small hidden room inside the main pantry. After pulling down a set of cabinets on the kitchen side of the wall, they expected to find a set of studs, but instead found the side frame work to a door. After a little investigation the hidden room was revealed.

Paul told Aimee it was probably used as a wine cellar when the house was originally built, but by the looks of it now, it was some type of food storage area.

Aimee loved the thought of a hidden room and decided to focus her morning on the room's contents. With the use of a lantern for additional light, Aimee began removing small bottles whose dried contents had been sealed within them by a cork and wax. The amount of dust and cobwebs made Aimee think this particular room had not been disturbed since the original Stuart sisters lived here.

There were multiple mortars and pestles which she thought might be things to take to the local antique store. She also found several books that contained recipes, or at least in the dimly-lit room that is what she thought. Aimee placed everything in a box, sealed it and wrote "Secret Pantry" on the top.

Once she moved into the house she would have plenty of time to study the contents of what she was packing up today. With the items she wanted to save out of the pantry, Aimee began hauling broken dishes and jars of very old preserves and other debris out to the dumpster. She could have left all of this to the crew since she was paying them, but found it fun to be part of the project.

As noon drew near Aimee tossed the last box of debris. "Paul, I am headed into town for lunch and to get a spare key made for you. I'll be back in a bit. Do you need anything?"

"No, we are fine, but thanks for asking."

As Aimee sat at the main traffic light leading into town she realized she was filthy. Her clothes were covered in thick dust and her hands were too dirty to go into a restaurant. The town's residents were already watching her for stress signs of living in a haunted house; she didn't want to make them think she was a slob as well, so she decided to stop at the hotel first and clean up.

The hotel was a beautiful Victorian structure built at the end of the 1800's. According to their website, they too have a few ghosts which have been reported by staff and guests alike over the years. Aimee wondered why the locals were okay with the hotel's ghosts but not with the ones that supposedly resided in her new home. She began to wonder if there was more to the story then she had heard. It was definitely something she would research once she had the house restored and more free time on her hands, but for now she needed to cleanup and get something to eat.

After lunch Aimee headed over to City Hall to apply for the electrical and plumbing permits. Mrs. Conway informed her it would be 14 days before she could pick them up and that she was not to start the upgrade until she had them posted on the front window of the house. Since the contractors had just started the removal of the walls and flooring; Aimee seriously doubted they would even be ready for the next stage in 14 days.

While at City Hall Aimee asked if it was possible to get a legal plat description of the land that she purchased and if they had any documentation about the house itself, from when it was originally constructed. She was hoping to learn about any additional secret rooms or hidden wells on the property.

Mrs. Conway told Aimee there might be something in archives but it would take time to research, and Aimee agreed to check back with her in 14 days when she picks up her permits.

Paul was sitting on the front porch when Aimee returned. "Here's a spare key for you guys," she said handing him the key. "So, what are you working on?" she said, leaning in to see what was on the screen of his laptop.

"I thought we could get a rough idea of what you want in your new kitchen while the guys finish cleaning up the debris, so I'm plugging in the measurements from the kitchen and pantry."

"If possible, I would like to keep the secret room. Don't know what I will use it for, but it is pretty cool," she said.

"Do you want to enlarge the kitchen?" Paul asked.

"Not really. I like the space usage in the house as it is. I think it would be a shame to start altering its original footprint. Let's just update the kitchen with granite, stainless steel, new cupboards, windows, etc. If the wooden floors in the house are worth saving I would love to sand and re-stain them."

"Well, keeping the rooms the same will definitely speed up the project, and our goal is to restore as much as possible, but we may need to replace a board here and there."

"That sounds great! I've been saving pictures from magazines on different kitchen designs that I like. I'll bring those tomorrow and then you can create a design idea from there."

Fall 1867 ~ Port Townsend

It was a lovely fall afternoon in 1867. Sitting quietly in his study, listening to the fire crackle, Lord Stuart's thoughts began to wander back in time, to a different perfect life. Mary was alive and their daughters were learning the essentials required of all well-bred young ladies: needlework, music and dance. It was during this blissful time he discovered his wife's dark secret and was not sure he could cope with it, or allow his children to be raised anywhere near it.

Mary assured him that her activities were merely a trending fascination, like those of many prominent Victorian women, and nothing more. Lord Stuart loved his wife and blindly believed her, until that fateful day when he found her lifeless body.

Mary's lovely features were forever frozen in a look of sheer terror, a look that still haunted his dreams. Lord Stuart knew he did the right thing by relocating his children from Scotland to Port Townsend.

After the death of his beloved wife, Mary, Lord William Stuart emigrated from Scotland to Port Townsend in 1851 with his three young daughters; Eliza, age 13, Jane, age 11 and Clair, age 9. He adamantly believed the only way to protect the girls was to remove them from the environment that took their mother. Selling what he could and leaving the remainder behind, Lord Stuart boarded the ship in Glasgow with nothing more than a desire to start over with his daughters and their Governess, in a safe new world. The girls, however, brought a secret.

Lord Stuart allowed his daughters to pack one large trunk with their favorite books and toys; instructing them that the remainder would be left behind for whomever wanted it. While Jane and Clair focused on their father's instructions and gathered the items, Eliza retrieved her mother's book of spells. Eliza carefully cut each page from the book and then, with her sisters' help, she pulled back the lining from the trunk and they hid the pages between the lining and the trunk walls and bottom. Once Lord Stuart had approved of the items that they wanted to keep, he allowed them to be placed inside the empty trunk. Then he instructed Lambert to lock the trunk in order to prevent any unwanted items from creeping in.

Lord Stuart maintained his title until the end of his life. The locals of Port Townsend recognized his unspoken authority and respected his honesty and fair treatment. By the summer of 1856 the Stuart Mansion had been completed on the bluff overlooking Port Townsend and Admiralty Bay. The Stuart Estate consisted of one-hundred acres with a grand home and a beautiful view. Lord Stuart planted several orchards of apples, cherries and peaches. The berry gardens contained raspberries, blackberries and blueberries while the vegetable gardens grew everything else. His daughters maintained an extensive herb garden next to the back of the house and they planted bed after bed of fragrant flowers to display inside the home. Some of his favorites included lavender, jasmine and honeysuckle. He hired many locals to work the land and he paid them all well. As his land prospered, so did the town of Port Townsend.

He promised himself his daughters would never know the truth about their mother's death and hoped he could free them from her terrible fascination.

Picking up a letter that had arrived for him earlier that day from his dear and trusted friend, John Wilson, Lord Stuart opened it and began to read. John was writing to inform William that Ashborne Manor was no longer suitable for anyone to live in. Shortly after their departure from Scotland, the property was leased to a wealthy family from Edinburgh. However, within a month, two of their children had died in garish accidents and the demonic rumors began to circulate in the local community and even made their way to the social circle in Glasgow. Since then, anyone who attempts to live there is either brutally attacked or found dead. The stench that began shortly after the initial incident, now consumes the entire structure and no one dares step foot on the Estate, let alone live in the Manor.

Lord Stuart was now convinced he had made the right decision when he left everything behind and brought his children to Port Townsend. He would sacrifice everything, all over again, if it meant protecting his daughters from their mother's ugly secret. But then logic started to take hold of his mind and a fear began to grip his heart.

Why were his daughters still single? What was their reason for turning down suitors, for always staying close to each other and never allowing anyone to intrude on their privacy? Was it possible that he had been so blind with his love for Mary that he believed her when she said their daughters were not aware of her secret? Did they know, were they truly their mother's daughters?

If he was to find the truth he knew right where to look. The girls had been insistent on having a secret hiding place that was only accessible from the third-floor nursery. They said it would remind them of their home in Scotland and all of the hiding places they had there. Wanting to please his daughters, he ordered the room to be built. It was well hidden in the wall and only someone who knew what to look for would find the mechanism to open the panel.

The girls were now far too old for the nursery or a secret room, but there were many times over the years when he would catch them coming down the stairs from the top floor. They would say they were simply reminiscing about their childhood and all the wonderful hours they spent in the nursery with their Governess, learning their lessons and playing with their toys.

Reaching the top floor, Lord Stuart walked the full length of the hallway, passing each servant's room as he headed to the front end of the house and the nursery. When he opened the door he noticed nothing unusual, just a meticulously clean room and all their childhood items, which they brought with them from Scotland, were displayed with great pride. Running his hand down the right side of the fireplace mantel, just under the third Scottish Thistle, he found the tiny lever and pressed; a panel in the side wall then popped open. Pushing the panel aside he realized his worst nightmare was true. His daughters were just like their mother.

In a fit of rage and terror, he turned quickly from the room and headed to the second floor main landing. It was then that he was overtaken by a violent pain in his left arm that reached through his chest and gripped his heart. Clutching his chest and arm with his right hand, he stumbled forward and fell down the grand staircase, finally, crashing at the bottom in a heap.

The sound reverberated throughout the house, bringing the servants and his daughters running. Clair was the first to reach her father, who lay motionless on the floor. She ordered a servant to ride into town and bring back the doctor.

Jane left her father's side and raced to the landing to see what caused the fall but found nothing. She wondered what he was doing up stairs. Climbing to the third floor, she soon realized that he had been in the nursery and opened the hidden panel. Pulling the panel shut and closing the nursery door, she then went back down to stay with her sisters until the doctor arrived.

While the doctor examined Lord Stuart, the sisters waited in the front parlor, huddled closely together by the fire.

"He knows," Jane whispered. "He opened the hidden panel and looked inside the room. He must have been rushing down the stairs when he fell."

"Let's not say anything right now. We will figure out what to say to Father once he is better," Eliza stated.

Eventually the doctor emerged, telling them Lord Stuart had suffered a stroke and lost his ability to speak. There was a slim chance he would regain it, but still, a very slim chance. In addition, he was paralyzed on his left side and he would now require their constant attention. The doctor offered to get in touch with a hospital in Seattle to see if a nurse could be hired to tend for him, but the sisters refused.

From that fateful day forward, his heart filled with terror, instead of love, every time he was left alone with his daughters. Lord Stuart lived another six months. A family cemetery was designed next to the berry gardens in the back yard. Lord William Stuart, Beloved Husband and Father, became the first resident.

Present Day ~ Port Townsend

The first 14 days of deconstruction flew by and Aimee was headed back to City Hall to pick up the plumbing and electrical permits. When she arrived at the office, Mrs. Conway was waiting for her with a small tube.

Sliding it across the counter she stated, "I did an extensive search for you, but not much is left of the original Stuart purchase. I did find an old plat that shows the house with your current orchards, the berry gardens and the cemetery, but nothing that dates back to its original purchase. I am sorry."

"Cemetery, there's a cemetery on my property!?"

"Yes, it is where Lord Stuart and his three daughters are buried."

"Wow, I never saw that one coming! Cool, I am going to have to get a weed whacker and start cutting down the forest of growth in the backyard to find it. But the best part, the original owner of my house, was a Lord!"

Mrs. Conway was shocked that Aimee was taking the news of a cemetery on her property so well. She figured it would be the final act that sent her running back to Boise.

As soon as Aimee got back to the house and posted the permits in the front window, she had to find Paul and tell him about the cemetery. He did not seem surprised and she figured that to him, cemeteries and ghosts were just part of these old homes.

Two additional crews joined the restoration project over the next three weeks. One focused on plumbing and the other on the electrical. When it was completed she was not only up to code, but had a water softener, central heat and A/C, surround sound, and a high-tech security system; although none of them worked yet.

Aimee was really feeling like the house was becoming her own when Paul unveiled her new gourmet kitchen and double pantry. She couldn't wait to get the entire place done so she could move out of the hotel. Then she would have time to look through all the boxes she had packed up from the different rooms and she could spend time working on the growth in the back yard. She was very eager to find the cemetery and to see if the berry garden was still producing.

The thought of weeding the property and removing what looked like a hundred years of over-growth was too daunting. So back to the internet to search for a landscape company that could start the work. Aimee loved to garden and tend plants, but the labor-intensive process of getting this garden ready really did require multiple people with the right equipment.

Surprisingly, she found a landscaper in Port Townsend who didn't have issues with doing work at the Stuart Mansion; as long as it was outside of the house and during daylight hours. Aimee laughed after she got off the phone with them. Nothing had happened to her or the Fredrickson crew and they were in the house at all hours of the day. Regardless, she was thrilled to have someone local to do the work. She thought it might improve the property's standing in the community if a reputable local resident could relay back to all interested parties, which was basically the entire town that in fact nothing odd happens at the Stuart Mansion.

First thing the next morning, Landscapes by Design arrived at the house and Aimee met the crew in the front yard.

"Let's just do the basics right now," she said, "remove weeds and all the under-growth. Once the chaos is gone, we can decide what plants and trees need to go or stay. If you need anything, just give me a ring on my cell phone and I'll come out and we can talk." Aimee was trying to ease the tension the crew might be feeling about being so close to a haunted house. She thought if she honored their wishes about always being outside, they might eventually forget their childish fears and they might actually enjoy working here, just like the Fredrickson crew does.

"Oh, I almost forgot," Aimee said as she turned around on the porch, "If you could focus the work around the house first and then spread out from there it would be helpful. The new windows will be installed in a few days and once that is done, a contractor will be here to scrape paint and power-wash the exterior before the house receives a new coat of paint."

Within three days, Aimee was able to see the entire house, from foundation to roof line, now that all the years of old growth had been removed. There was so much of it that Aimee obtained a burning permit so the landscapers could create a fire pit to burn the branches and debris as they went. Once the house was cleared they moved outward, clearing everything to the property line on both sides of the house and the front section.

It took the landscapers several weeks to clear the debris at the rear of the property and finally reach the family cemetery. It was located approximately 300 yards from the back of the house. A large oak tree anchored the space and a black wrought-iron fence enclosed four headstones within its perimeter. Aimee knew she wanted to be the first one to enter the little cemetery through its small gate, and lovingly clear away the weeds and branches. She felt like an archaeologist about to enter the newly-discovered tomb of a great Pharaoh and wanted to protect it from the workers who did not understand the importance of their discovery. Her intention was to create four small flower beds in front of each tombstone and plant an assortment of flowers. She would fill the rest of the area in with heavy gravel to keep weeds down and show the cemetery the respect it deserved.

Aimee was surprised to find there were actually five graves in the tiny cemetery. The fifth grave was marked by a small flat stone that read 'Our Loving Cousin Corporal Martin Samuel Stuart 1870.' Aimee had no idea who this cousin was; no one had mentioned a second man living at the house, just the father and his three daughters. Aimee saw this as another mystery to investigate once she was settled into the house.

The landscapers arrived early the next morning to pour a decorative concrete bed border around each headstone, providing her an enclosed area to grow the flowers and another way to keep the cemetery tidy. Even without the gravel or any plants Aimee thought the space looked very peaceful and decided to purchase a couple of stone angels to watch over the Stuarts.

A natural stone path was laid that led from the back door of the house to the cemetery. The path had several turns and bends to give it a more natural feel. Aimee wanted to place a bench and a pond along the path as well to create a park-like setting.

Aimee also decided to keep the original layout of the herb beds that were located just outside the back door. The landscapers suggested erecting a fence around the space to help keep the wildlife out, although nothing was going to be 100% effective. It was impossible to tell what had been planted where, but the beds were bordered with large stones so it was just a matter of tilling the soil inside each bed and starting over. She liked the idea of keeping the stones and the layout; if it was good enough for the Stuart family, it was good enough for her.

To the right of the back door, facing towards the cemetery, there were remnants of vast flower gardens. In one spot wild roses had taken over and the lavender had gone wild but continued to grow in small patches. It was decided to clear the soil and till in a good fertilizer, then look at planting next spring. The ground had been neglected for so long that it really needed time to heal before she could begin her own flower beds. Aimee didn't mind, she wanted time to plan out the garden so it would provide her with years of enjoyment.

Spring 1848 ~ Scotland

Mr. Lambert, Lord Stuart's personal Valet and Butler, rushed into the Library without his customary knock, pause and slow opening of the door. Lord Stuart looked up in surprise at this unusual break from tradition and realized he had never seen Lambert look so flustered.

"Sir," Mr. Lambert began, trying to catch his breath, "something is happening in the closed portion of the North Wing."

"What do you mean 'happening'? Has someone broken in?"

"I'm not sure, Sir, but one of the gardeners reported the windows blew outward and glass landed on him. He also claims he heard multiple people screaming."

"You stay here, Lambert; I'll go take a look."

Ashborne Manor had been the Stuart family home since the early 14th Century. The last major additions were completed in 1740 by William Adam and, subsequently, his sons. The North Wing was closed off nearly fifty years ago after a fire and, because it was no longer safe, plans were underway to tear it down and have a new addition built. No one had access to the closed section besides himself, Lambert and Nathaniel.

Lord Stuart thought he had experienced some horrific things in his life, but when he reached the North Wing and opened the door to the old Morning Room, he was frozen in horror by what greeted him. All of the windows had been shattered outward, just as the gardener described. The entire room was destroyed, as if an explosion had taken place.

A low moaning could be heard from within the room, and he moved quickly into the destruction to find what or who was making the sound. On the far side of the room he found his brother Nathaniel, pinned under a stone pillar from the massive fireplace. Following the direction his brother's hand was pointing, Lord Stuart found his wife, pinned to the wall with a metal post driven through her stomach. Quickly scanning the room, looking for the assailant, he immediately realized it was Mary's harmless flirtation, as she put it, with magic that caused this. He could see portions of a pentagram on the floor with candles and overturned bowls. Turning his attention back to Nathaniel, he tried to comfort him in his last moment.

"I'm sorry, William," he said. "I begged her to do it for me."

"Shh, nothing can be done now," Lord Stuart said, stroking Nathaniel's hair away from his eyes.

"Something came out of the darkness, it was horrible…," Nathaniel began, but it was too late for him; the weight of the stone finally pushed out his last breath. Lord Stuart knelt by his brother for a few moments, then he closed Nathaniel's eyes for the last time. Standing, he slowly walked towards his wife, where he kissed his fingers and placed them on her lips before gently closing her eyes. Taking a deep breath he turned away from the carnage and headed out of the room, closing and locking the door behind him. What had Nathaniel begged his wife to do and more so, what demonic creature had been released into their home?

Lord Stuart directed Lambert to send for the Master of Police and two of his most trusted Police Constables. He would wait for them in his Library, and absolutely no one was to enter the closed off section of the house.

A knock on the Library door told Lord Stuart that Lambert was back with the Master of Police and his men.

"Come in, John," he said. He and John Wilson had been friends since their early days at Oxford. John had always had an inquisitive mind and was perfectly suited for his position, while Lord Stuart also knew that his place was to be the next Earl of Ashborne Manor. There were many times at University when he thought John had the better lot in life. He was free to choose his path.

"William, what is going on here? Your man refused to tell me anything beyond the fact that you had an emergency that required my immediate attention."

"I'm sorry, John, but I cannot allow word of this to go beyond these walls. After I show you what I discovered, you can decide if your Constables should be included or not."

Mr. Lambert led the way through the main building and hallways of the closed section until the group was standing outside the locked Morning Room.

"Prepare yourself, John," Lord Stuart said as he opened the door and the two men slipped inside.

"Good Lord William, what in hell happened here!?"

"Just before Nathaniel died he said he begged Mary to do this, to perform magic or whatever it's called. He said something evil came through."

"Came through what?" John asked, looking around.

"John, Mary had a secret when I married her. She was descended from powerful witches, as was her mother, and her mother before her, and back as far as time can record. They belonged to a Coven in Edinburgh. She told me that she had broken from the Coven because they practiced the dark arts and she was only interested in tarot cards and séances."

"By the look of this William, she was involved in far more than tarot cards."

Lord Stuart directed his friend to where his brother lay and then over to where his wife was impaled on the wall.

"John, I don't know how to handle this. If any of this gets out I will be ruined, I will have to relinquish my seat in the House. My daughters will be rejected by society, their lives will be ruined."

"William, I don't see how you will be able to avoid scandal. I think what we need to decide is, which type of scandal will be easiest to recover from. This," he said waving his hand in a circle in front of them, "can never be recovered from."

"Let's discuss this in the privacy of your library, William," John stated. Locking the door behind them, Mr. Lambert led the group back down to the Library. The Master of Police released his Constables back to their regular duties. Lambert poured the two men a drink and then retired from the Library to let them speak in private.

"Bottom line, William, this incident as it currently stands will destroy you and everyone around you. However, if we report that your wife and brother have left Scotland for parts unknown, you will have gossip but nothing you cannot recover from."

"That's all fine and good, John, but what do we do about the mess in the Morning Room?"

"Well, we cannot bury them in the Churchyard; they have been touched by evil. I do have a contact at the Edinburgh Medical School; they are always looking for legal ways to obtain cadavers for research."

"Good God man! I cannot turn my wife and brother over to those butchers. No, I refuse to accept that as a solution!"

"If you are willing to include your Butler, we could bury them in the Pauper's Cemetery after dark, but it will take the three of us. They would rest there in an unmarked grave, but at least they will be buried."

"Damn, John, I don't like any of these solutions, but considering what we are dealing with I believe your last option is the best. I will convey everything to Lambert and we will be waiting for your return about ten o'clock this evening."

"Alright, William, I will make arrangements with the caretaker to dig a grave. The ground is pretty well thawed and he will easily get a double dug by tonight."

"What do you mean a 'double'? They need separate graves!"

"William, paupers are buried in mass graves; not individual ones which are reserved for Churchyards. I'm sorry dear friend, but to keep any questions from arising, it must appear that two paupers are dead and being buried as usual."

Lord Stuart knew his friend was right, but it went against his moral fiber to place his beloved wife and brother in a grave for all eternity, together. "Very well, John, let me walk you out."

"Lambert, I need to speak to you in private," Lord Stuart said as he turned and headed back to his Library. Lambert followed close behind. Once inside the room, Lord Stuart asked him to sit in the chair next to his. Pouring and handing a glass of whiskey to Lambert, Lord Stuart informed him that what he was about to hear was very tragic and surely would be upsetting. As the description of what was discovered in the Morning Room and the details involved to cover up the horrible incident were laid before him, Lord Stuart could see the color drain from Lambert's face and, at the same time, he could see the man sit taller and straighter.

"Yes, Sir," Lambert replied, "you can depend on me. My family has been serving your family for five generations and I will not let either of our families down at a time like this."

"Good man, Lambert," Lord Stuart said, as he extended his hand to shake Lambert's.

"Well, we had better get some blankets and ropes to cover them with and head back to the room so we can be ready when John returns," Lord Stuart stated.

Standing outside the locked door, Lord Stuart placed his hand on Lambert's shoulder, "Prepare yourself," he said.

Allowing Lambert a moment to take in the destruction and regain his bearings, Lord Stuart then led him over to the stone pillar that had crushed Nathaniel.

"Grab one of those beams and wedge it under the pillar, just there and I'll do one about here," Lord Stuart said as he pointed at two different sections of the pillar.

"If we can leverage the beams properly, we should be able to rock the stone and get it to roll off his chest."

Several minutes later the pillar began to move and the two men were able to free Nathaniel's trapped body from beneath it. Lambert picked up one of the blankets and laid it over the crushed body.

Picking up the ropes, Lambert walked over to where Lady Stuart was impaled to the wall. Handing one rope to Lord Stuart, Lambert firmly tied his end to the metal post and then did the same with the remaining rope. Each man, taking one rope, stretched their rope till it was taut and then began to pull with all their might. Very slowly, the post began to retreat from the wall and, with one final pull, they freed Lady Stuart. In the process they fell backwards onto the rubble, once the post broke free of the wall and her body. Lady Mary Stuart fell with a thud to the floor. Lambert grabbed the remaining quilt and covered her body while Lord Stuart regained his composure from the tumble he took. With each body securely wrapped in the quilts and tied with the ropes, the two men retreated back to the main house, where they occupied their time until the Master of Police returned.

Mr. Lambert instructed the staff on their specific evening duties to ensure that no one would be in the areas of the main house when he, Lord Stuart and the Master of Police came through with the bodies. By midnight, both bodies were in the back of a wagon and the three men rode in silence through the dark night to the other side of Glasgow, where they would forever say goodbye to Nathaniel and Lady Stuart. Dawn was beginning to break when they finally returned to Ashborne.

Within a few days the entire County knew of the affair between Lady Stuart and Nathaniel. Gossip ran rampant at afternoon teas, the Opera House and any other location where bored women gathered.   Lord Stuart was above reproach from the rumors and his position in society kept him relatively free from any damage it would have caused a less important man. However, he feared for his daughters' good names. A scandal like this could reduce their chances to form good matches and marry well. He did not have a male heir, so everything he owned would be entailed away upon his death, leaving them penniless unless they married well. His only saving thought was that the girls were still very young and much of this would hopefully be a vague memory by the time they are introduced into society.

For a time, life seemed to return to normal around Ashborne, until the day one of the upstairs maids, caught up in her fear and screams, missed the top stair and plummeted to the bottom of the marble staircase, breaking her neck. An investigation into what she could have possibly encountered on the second floor began, but nothing was discovered.   Pungent odors began to overtake rooms and they were eventually closed off when no amount of cleaning could free them of the foul stench. Servants started whispering about being watched and hearing a low growling noise as they moved through the day completing their tasks. Certain areas of the house were no longer worked by one servant alone; they went in pairs or groups so someone could keep watch.

Spring 1870 ~ Port Townsend

"Eliza; would you like a cup of tea before Clair and I head into town to get the rest of our supplies?" Jane asked.

"Yes, that would be lovely, dear," she replied.   Eliza volunteered to stay with their injured cousin; she felt it her duty as the eldest Stuart. "I will relay any information if he should wake."

The servants were dismissed several years back and now the house seemed strangely quiet once Jane and Clair had departed for town. Eliza could hear the clock in the hall and the sound of the wind as it swirled around the outside of the house, but Martin did not stir. She wondered if the three of them had the ability to save him. His wounds were deep and he had lost a lot of blood. They did discuss calling for the doctor, but knew they had powers far beyond his medical experience to save Martin's life, and once the town got involved they would be unable to help.

The grandfather clock struck one when Jane and Clair returned from town. Clair was excited to tell Eliza what they had heard in the store. It seems two strangers were asking about the Stuarts yesterday and the bartender drew them a map to reach the mansion. Unfortunately they never made it because crew members from the Windspur abducted them.

Well, at least they now know what happened. One man escaped, barely, and his friend was now forced labor on the ship.

"We were able to get everything we needed Eliza," Jane said.

"You didn't say anything about this man did you?" Eliza asked, already knowing the answer.

"Of course not," was Jane's reply.

"Clair, if you wouldn't mind sitting in here for a bit, I need to stretch my legs and prepare the ointment to re-wrap his wounds," Eliza stated as she stood and walked towards the door.

"Jane, why don't you place a bit of last night's broth on the stove to warm. He might wake while we are changing his dressings," Eliza said.

As Eliza worked on the ointment, she and Jane discussed what was left to complete for Friday's full moon ceremony. They also discussed if they should attempt to save his life, or allow nature to run its course and obviously what it meant to them, if they did save his life.

"The ointment is ready, Jane. Will you bring the broth and help me change his dressings?" Eliza asked as she headed back into the bedroom.

"Clair, will you grab the clean dressings and assist us?" Jane asked of her sister. The three women took great care when moving Martin onto his sides so they could remove the soaked dressings. Their actions were methodic and loving, taking the greatest of care not to inflict any additional pain. Once they had the new wraps in place on the bed, he was laid on his bac, allowing Eliza to cover each wound with her special ointment while Clair assisted Jane with securing the dressings over the wounds. They had nearly completed their task when he opened his eyes and blinked a few times trying, to focus on his surroundings and the women hovering over him.

"Jane, bring the broth and try to get him to take a bit," Eliza said as she motioned towards the cup on the side table. Eliza and Clair jointly assisted him in lifting his head up so he could take a sip of the broth.

"It hurts," he whispered.

"Clair, run get the Laudanum; we can give him a bit of that to ease the pain," Eliza said.

"Martin, we are not going to lie to you, your wounds are very deep and you have lost a lot of blood. Only God knows what his plans are for you at this point," Eliza said, looking down at him with a gentle smile.

"It's not fair that my family line ends with me. I've let my parents down…," he began, but then started coughing up blood and could no longer continue.

"Hush, just rest dear boy. We will do all that is within our power to save you," Eliza said as she poured a small amount of Laudanum into his mouth. "Just rest."

"Sisters, shall we retire to the kitchen and let him rest a bit? I think it's time to prepare our supper," Eliza said, motioning for them to leave the room with a gentle sweep of her hand. Once safely in the kitchen and away from Martin's hearing, Eliza told Clair that she and Jane had discussed the possibility of them saving his life, but that they knew there would be a great cost for doing it. Clair agreed with her sisters that this was what they were meant to do. Everyone is placed on earth for a purpose and they now believed their true purpose had been revealed.

"So Eliza, how are we going to ensure that our work is not undone after we are gone? So many things could go wrong and we would not be around to explain anything," Clair asked.

"Well, we will have to plan this out very carefully, think of every possible outcome and how we can ensure his survival. I also believe it must be completed on Friday for it to be successful. Do we all agree?" Eliza asked.   It was unanimous; they would do everything in their power to save their cousin Martin Stuart.

****

Clair had always been the most creative of the Stuart sisters. She was the one who came up with the idea of getting father to build them a secret room; she knew how to deter all the suitors who came their way, and she was the one who came up with the final plan.

Over the next few days they would take turns repeating a message to Martin and making sure that he has it memorized. They would drill into him the importance of never forgetting the message. So every opportunity they had, whether he was awake or not, they would tell him: *"Guard the children's memories -- Wait for her love to free you."* Just to be safe, they would also write the message on pieces of paper and pin them to every wall in the house.

When Eliza opened the front door she found her sisters pushing the settee across the foyer and into the dining room. She was surprised at how much furniture they had cleared from the parlor while she was in town.

"Jane, why don't you and Clair take a break; I'll put the kettle on and we can have afternoon tea. I bought some lovely treats at the bakery," she said as she took off her jacket and bonnet.

"Did you speak with Mr. Turner?" Jane asked as they walked into the kitchen.

"Yes. I've taken care of my Will and he is expecting the two of you to stop by on Thursday to redo yours and sign them," Eliza said as she placed the box with the bakery treats on the table and reached for the kettle.

"He didn't think it odd?" Clair asked.

"A bit, but I let him believe it was just the wishes of three old spinsters and that we wouldn't be able to sleep at night until this matter was cleared up."

"Eliza, you are terrible," Clair laughed.

"Well, at least we have guaranteed the safety of the house and the primary land. Let's just hope it doesn't take too long for everything else to fall into place. I would hate to think Martin has to wait two or three years for this to work," Jane commented.

"I'm sure it won't Jane. Once the Stuart family knows the house and land are theirs if they live here, someone will definitely show up to claim their right to the property. Then there will be laughter and social events and lots of beautiful women," Eliza said as she tossed another log into the stove to fuel the fire for the kettle.

As they enjoyed their afternoon tea the sisters discussed the weather and what the Seattle fashions might be in the summer and fall. They checked on Martin, who although very weak, was sleeping soundly. To them it was just another day and the approach of a very special Friday.

The days both dragged on relentlessly and flew by at the same time for the sisters. The life they were trying to save in the guest bedroom was slipping away faster than the hours were passing, yet they had many preparations to complete and events had to be put into place for their plan to work.

Eliza busied herself with gathering all their loose spells and recording them in their spell book; once done, she wrapped the book in several layers of cloth and readied it for her sisters to hide. She also gathered all the personal belongings that Martin had with him, to include the small bag of gold coins and several pieces of jewelry, and placed that with the book of spells.

Jane baked pies and breads for the next few days. She was always happiest when she was cooking and creating sumptuous dishes. She compiled all her favorite recipes and placed them in a box inside the secret pantry, hoping that someone would enjoy preparing them in the future.

Clair had to clean the house, dust every room and tidy every shelf. Her passions were herbs and flowers. The Spring Lilies were just beginning to bloom and she filled the vases with fresh cuttings.

Present Day ~ Port Townsend

Christmas was Aimee's favorite time of year. With Thanksgiving only two weeks away, she was eagerly awaiting the delivery of all the new Christmas decorations she had ordered and for the local garden center to call her when their stock of Christmas trees arrived. With her home restoration completed, she planned to host Christmas for family and friends and show off her new place.

Just as she looked up from her laptop she saw the delivery truck drive past the window and knew that they were making the first of many deliveries. Rushing downstairs, she met them at the door.

"Good morning," the driver said, "we have quite a few packages for you. Will you start signing here, and they go down to here," he said as he drew a single line for her to sign on, that covered all the packages.

"Happily," she said. "What's Christmas without all the trimming and decorations? I just moved in and this is my first holiday here," she commented as she handed the clipboard back to the driver.

"Where would you like me to place them?"

"You can set them in the foyer. I'll sort through them there." Aimee laughed to herself. She really did have a lot of packages. How much did she order!?

The last ones to come inside were marked: Perishable Open Immediately. She could tell from the decal on the boxes that they were the lavender wreaths she ordered for the front door and windows. She discovered the lavender farms in Sequim earlier in the summer and placed her holiday wreath order at that time. Lavender was her favorite aromatherapy scent and she thought it would really add a special touch to the season.

Carefully removing the wreaths and laying them on the floor, she counted 20 window wreaths and one large door wreath. Now she needed to figure out which boxes had the hooks and flameless candles. Her plan was to place a single candle in each window, centered below the wreath. The best part of the candles: they came with a remote! She only needed to stand in the room and click the remote and they turned on, versus turning 20 on each night and off each morning. Technology was great.

Once all the boxes were opened and their contents carefully placed on the floor, Aimee began to sort the ornaments that would go on the tree in the living room, the ones for the tree in the dining room and the rest would go on the tree that would be set up on the second floor landing. Each fireplace would have a garland of fresh evergreen bows and pine cones, with more of the flameless candles. She planned to weave a silk poinsettia garland the full length of the stair case railings and along each landing. She had purchased two life-size reindeer decorations and a life-size Victorian Santa, but they were not in this delivery. She planned to place them in the foyer, along with a fresh-flocked tree, to greet everyone.

Over the next two weeks, Aimee became good friends with the delivery men. One delivered in the AM and another in the PM; she could almost set her clock by the deliveries.

Aimee planned to spend the day prior and Thanksgiving Day

with her sister Sarah and her husband Peter in Seattle, and then return midday on Friday so she would be ready to start decorating her trees once they arrived Saturday morning.

The knock on the front door told Aimee that the taxi was there to take her to the ferry dock. Sarah was going to meet her at the other end and brave the crazy holiday travelers so Aimee wouldn't have to drive. With a last glance around the house, Aimee set the security alarm and clicked the remote to turn off the wireless candles. Locking the door behind her, she handed her bag to the driver and got into the cab.

"This will be my first winter in Port Townsend. Do you think we will have snow?" she asked the driver.

"It's rare for us to get snow here because we are so close to the saltwater. However, we have been known to get a good three inches in as little as two hours. You never know, this may be another one of those rare snow years," he replied.

"Oh, I hope so. It would be so lovely to have all logs burning in the fireplaces, then look out towards the Bay and see snow coming down. I'm a romantic, I know," she said.

"Well, you can still have the fires burning and look out toward the Bay, but I doubt you will see it because of the fog," he chuckled.

"Yes, we have had several weeks of that, haven't we?"

The ferry ride was a little rough and with all the fog Aimee couldn't focus her eyes on the horizon to keep her stomach steady. When they finally reached the port in Seattle, she was the first in line to walk on solid land.

"Hi, sweetie," Sarah said as she gave Aimee a hug. "How was the trip?"

"Horrible, I thought I was going to be remembered like the passengers on the Titanic!"

"You are such a wimp, Aimee. It couldn't be that bad."

"No, it was just really bumpy; but you know me, always freaked out around deep bodies of water."

"Then why do you torture yourself by taking the ferry?" Sarah asked.

"Because it is the fastest way to get here from Port Townsend, and I'd rather spend my time shopping in the Market before we head to your place, not driving the long route to get here."

"When we get home, Peter has a surprise for you," Sarah said with a smile.

"Oh, please tell me he hasn't invited more of his single friends over. I'm still recovering from the last one."

"No. I made him promise to stop doing that. Actually, he did something for you because he knew you would be too busy getting your house decorated for the holidays, and wouldn't have time to do it yourself."

"What?" Aimee asked.

"You will just have to wait until we get done shopping," she replied.

"Now you are just being cruel; Sarah."

Aimee loved to shop and have girl time, but she loved

surprises even more. With the anticipation of a surprise waiting for her when they got home, she found herself going through the stores faster and faster.

"A friend of my father's works for the Olympic Peninsula Historic Society," Peter said, handing a folder to Aimee. "I know you've been really busy with the house and now the holidays, so I took it upon myself to see if my Dad's friend could find any documentation on your new home."

"Peter; that was so thoughtful of you," she said, taking the folder.

"Well, Sarah said I needed to do something nice to make up for the bad dates I keep sticking you with," he laughed.

"Wow; there really is a lot of information here," she said as she opened the folder.

"Not sure how much is factual, or rumor. There are newspaper accounts and police reports along with city documents. In a nutshell, the house was built by a Lord Stuart who had three daughters. He died from complications due to a stroke and they, well, they were found dead in the front parlor, slumped over with a dead man between them. He had stab wounds in his stomach. Seems the sisters were witches," Peter said.

"Witches, are you serious?" Aimee looked at him like he was nuts.

"Well it was rumored, that they were performing a ritual the night they died. Maybe they are the ghosts that everyone says are haunting the place."

"I've been there nearly a year and neither I nor any of the construction crews had a single problem. I think the town gossip took sad deaths, and turned them into the new Salem Witch Hunt. I don't believe the house has any ghosts."

"I agree with you, Aimee," Peter said. "At least with this information and all the books and junk you stored away during the renovation you might be able to piece the whole thing together. Who knows, maybe even write a book about it and then it will be a movie and you will be famous and you can give me all the credit."

"Peter, you are hopeless!" Sarah said as she punched his arm.

"Oh, okay, you don't have to give me all the credit, but you will at least be able to defend your home."

****

The same driver who dropped Aimee off a few days earlier picked her up at the ferry dock upon her return.

"I see you did a bit of shopping," he said as he gathered all the bags and placed them in the trunk.

"Oh, just a tiny bit."

When they reached the Stuart Mansion, Aimee had the driver place the bags with her new treasures on the sofa while she disarmed the security system.

Handing the driver a tip, "I hope you have a wonderful holiday season, and thanks for the help."

"It was my pleasure."

****

Aimee was eager to read through the documents Peter gave her. Unsure of where to start, she grabbed a notepad and pen from the writing desk and wrote 'mysterious death of sisters' on the top half of the page and 'strange dead man' on the bottom half. She drew a line underneath the headings and started looking through the packet of papers. As she read through the old newspaper clippings, she wrote down any information that fell within those two categories. The top clipping started the ball rolling:

May 15, 1870: Once the heavy spring rains had stopped and the ground had ample time to dry enough for a horse to reach the Stuart Mansion in Port Townsend, local merchant Thomas Dew rode out to the Mansion to check on the Stuart sisters. Mr. Dew discovered the bodies of Eliza, Jane and Clair Stuart lying on the floor of their front parlor. The body of an unknown man was also discovered in the same room. Circumstances of their deaths are mysterious and foul play has not been ruled out. It was noted that the house was in pristine condition except for the parlor furniture being crowded into the dining room. Chief Ragsdale of the Seattle Police department has been contacted but will not arrive for a few days.

Aimee looked up from the clipping and glanced around her lovely living room, finding it difficult to imagine four dead bodies lying on this very floor over a hundred years ago. No wonder people gossiped about the house. Searching through the documents she found copies of the remaining news clippings pertaining to the deaths.

May 25, 1870: Seattle Authorities have ruled the cause of death involving the three Stuart sisters in Port Townsend as an occult suicide. Evidence was discovered that led investigators to believe the sisters were practicing black magic and the body of the young man has been identified as Martin Samuel Stuart, a first cousin. It is believed he was sacrificed prior to the triple suicide.

"Bloody Hell!" Aimee blurted out as she dropped the pages from her hand. "I need a drink!"

So many thoughts were racing through her mind as she entered the pantry and opened the hidden door to her wine cellar. All she could think of was that witches owned this house and murdered their cousin; but why?

Opening the wine and setting it on the serving tray, she grabbed a box of crackers and assortment of cheese from the fridge and she headed back to the parlor. Placing the tray on the side table, Aimee turned to sit on the sofa and that is when she saw it - the remote to the flameless candles propped up against the back of the seat cushion, but the batteries and back were missing. Not sure what was going on, she placed the remote on the table and reached for the wine bottle and glass. To her surprise, sitting on the tray were the batteries and the back cover to the remote.

"Seriously!" she said to no one in particular. "If you are trying to scare me so I will leave, you are wrong. This is my house and if you don't like it then you can leave!" Pouring a glass of wine and quickly drinking it, she put the remote back together and placed it on the table, popped a cracker with cheese in her mouth and continued to read the documents.

Nothing made sense to Aimee. Why would three sisters murder a cousin and then kill themselves? If it was black magic, what did they gain or cause to happen? In all the time that she had lived in the house not one strange or frightening thing had happened, well except for the remote and the batteries a few minutes ago. No, she just couldn't accept that whatever took place all those years ago was evil. There was nothing about this house that made her feel uncomfortable or nervous.

Aimee decided it was getting late and that she was going to need to spend a great deal of time investigating this matter before she said anything to anyone. Everything would just have to wait because tomorrow her live Christmas trees were arriving!

****

The Thanksgiving Holiday was over and everyone had returned to their daily routines. Aimee, however, knew today would be one of those days when you get to work, you immediately wish you were home in your cozy bed, with a roaring fire, watching the storm outside while you were comfy inside. That is exactly what Aimee planned to do, stay in bed and relax to the sounds of Mother

Nature and watch Mr. Darcy fight against his better judgment to not fall in love with Elizabeth Bennett.

Lying on her back with the pillows propping her up a bit, Aimee felt at peace with the world. The crackle of the fire and the patter of rain on the windows began to soothe her into a lazy sleep, when something in the bedroom doorway caught her attention.

Sitting up, she realized it was a man, and for whatever reason unknown to her conscious, she was not terrified. He simply stood there, in the ugliest, baggiest suit she had ever seen. It was too big and he reminded her of a little boy playing dress-up with his father's clothes. Her natural instinct forced her to push her back up against the headboard and pull the covers up to her chin.

"Who are you and how did you get in here?!" she demanded.

Before the man could answer, she quickly reached for the phone saying, "I'm calling the police and they will drag you out of here."

"Actually, you are the only one who can help me leave," he said, not moving from his spot.

"Fine, get the hell out!"

"I wish it was that easy Aimee, but I have a feeling it is going to be a lengthy and complex process."

"Who the hell are you!?" she demanded again. "And how do you know my name?"

"I'm Martin, the man who died downstairs."

"Yeah, right! Now I'm definitely calling the police," she said, bringing the phone up to dial the number but as she pressed the "9," she looked up and he was gone. "What the...?"

Quickly pushing the covers off, she jumped out of bed and before she could take two steps he reappeared, out of thin air and simply stood in front of her. That type of surprise was more than Aimee was prepared for and she fainted.

"Great, that went well," Martin said to no one as he sat on the floor next to where Aimee laid, passed out.

When Aimee came to she did not immediately understand why she was lying on the floor, but once she focused her eyes she saw the man sitting there, just watching her, and she remembered.

"Please, don't scream or do anything foolish, because I won't hurt you," he said.

Sitting up, Aimee scooted herself back towards the bed and away from the man. "Wow, I must have gotten up too quick and had a serious head rush to pass out like that."

"Actually, I think you passed out because you realized I am a ghost," he said as he faded away and then reappeared.

"Okay, you really have to stop doing that!"

Standing up and slowly backing herself back into bed, Aimee pulled the covers up to her chin and just stared at the man on the floor; who never moved.

"So, you have been here the entire time. Here, in this house, in my bedroom, in my bathroom!"

"Well, yes."

"You have, oh my god, you have been watching me. You pervert!"

"No," he said as he stood, "it is nothing like that."

"Okay then, tell me what spying on someone is like."

"One night, after you moved in, I heard this beautiful music and I followed it down to this room. When I entered it was dark but I could see a soft glow from behind that door," he said, pointing towards the bathroom. "I admit I stood at the door and just watched the peaceful expression on your face as you rested in the tub. That was the only time! I promise on the honor of the Stuart name: I am not an indecent man as you suggested."

"Let's back this low-budget horror movie up to the beginning. Well, your beginning. Why are you haunting my house, or better yet, why were you not haunting my house? I get the feeling you are just hanging out, probably watching movies with me and following me around for entertainment."

"Truth is, I have watched movies with you," he said with a grin. "I find them very fascinating. I especially enjoy the comedies; I cannot remember the last time I laughed so hard."

"What? You really have been hanging out with me, having a good time, and I didn't even know you were there? This is just wrong on so many levels."

"So, it was you who placed the remote on the sofa and the batteries on the tray?"

"Yes. I was trying to ease you into the idea of me, of a ghost, being in the house with you."

"Yeah, I don't really think you can ease someone into that scenario, but good try. So," Aimee said, relaxing her grip on the blankets, "why are you here?"

"Do you mind if I sit?" he asked, pointing to the end of the bed.

"Uh, I guess not."

Martin stood and walked to the bed, where he sat down at an angle facing her. Aimee could see him sitting firmly on the bed, but he did not affect the blankets or disturb the mattress with his weight.

"Comfy?" she asked.

"Yes, thanks," he said with a smile.

"So back to the million dollar question, why are you here?"

"My Uncle, Lord William Stuart, owned this house. My father, Fitzpatrick Stuart, was his youngest brother. I conveyed a letter of introduction from my father to my Uncle in hopes of securing work and starting a new life out here."

"Was Lord Stuart the father of Eliza, Jane and Clair Stuart?"

"Yes, they are my first cousins."

"Okay, so you get here with a letter and then what?"

"I never actually got the letter to my Uncle. To be honest, I remember very little after Henry and I stopped at the saloon to obtain directions here and have something to eat. We left the establishment and were attacked. They took Henry and I was stabbed several times trying to free him. Apparently, I made my way here and then I died."

"So, who was Henry?" Aimee asked.

"His family owned the farm next to ours and we would spend our time fishing and hunting together. I can still remember that winter when we were crossing the frozen lake near our property, and I stepped on a weak spot and fell into the freezing water. Henry risked his own life to save me, and we had been best friends since then. We also served in the Confederate Army together and again, he saved my life during a fierce battle after I had been shot and left for dead. Once the war was over, we decided to head out West with the letter of introduction to my Uncle, which my father left for me.

"Wow, that's a lot to take in. I am sorry about your friend though. Do you have any idea what could have happened to him?"

"Well, over the years as people came and went from the house, I gathered the town was having problems with ship Captains taking unwilling men as deck hands."

"Oh yeah, I remember seeing a TV special on that, but I think it was in Portland, Oregon."

"Yes, I saw that one with you."

Aimee had a strange look on her face and then shook her head. "Too weird!"

"What is weird?"

"You, a ghost, watching TV with me and now we are discussing the show like it was a really normal thing to do," she said with a chuckle.

"Okay, so back to you. You get here, never talk to the Uncle and then die. Do you remember meeting your cousins?"

"Yes, but only a little. They seemed very gentle and they took care of me."

"So, you don't remember them killing you?"

"No, they were kind and gentle. They would never have done that!" he said; standing and storming to the window. "I don't know how I died, but they did not kill me."

And then he vanished. No puff of smoke, or gust of wind. He simply wasn't there. Aimee got out of bed and wrapped a blanket around her shoulders. "Martin, I'm sorry. Please come back and talk with me."

She never found him. He was invisible again, somewhere within the house. He could see her and follow her movements, but she was not to know what he was doing.

****

The dawn could not wake Aimee since it was hidden behind the dark rain clouds. When she finally woke it was 8:30 AM, but felt like 6:30AM with the lack of sunlight. Leaning over to turn on the bed side lamp, she began to recall the events from the night prior. She had always told herself that if she moved into a haunted house she would not stay like all the people in the movies do. She would pack her things and be gone immediately. To Aimee, it seemed more like a dream than an actual event; perhaps it was a vivid dream that her mind created from the information she had read the two days prior.

Aimee decided to make a pot of coffee and spend the remainder of the morning working on the new business project she received before Thanksgiving. Then she would focus the remainder of the day sorting through all of the documents in the packet which Peter had given her.

Aside from the news clippings she read the night before, the only other intriguing information was that Eliza had contacted the family Solicitor three days prior to their death and had her Will changed. She left everything to Jane and Clair and stipulated that the house and the current five acres surrounding it remain intact and within the Stuart family forever. She also stipulated that the sale of the remaining acreage would be held in trust to support the house and five acres. Both Jane and Clair drew up Wills identical to Eliza's and signed them as well.

A promissory note was also signed and left for the undertaker so he could bury them next to their father and then place a small marker above each of their graves. They even requested a coffin and marker for their cousin, Martin. It was as if they were planning to die and wanted to protect everything before they went. But what were they protecting it for? They could have lived there for many years; they were not that old.

****

It's amazing what you can find on the internet. Within an hour of asking various questions on the web related to the sisters, the house and witchcraft, Aimee found a posting that showed a very old and faded picture of the crime scene, one of the dining room where all the furniture had been relocated, and another of a piece of paper that had a message written on it: *Guard the children's memories – Wait for her love to free you.*

The images were difficult to make out because the photos were peeling and looked like they had been folded several times. Aimee could see what appeared to be a man lying in the center of a pentagram and dozens of melted candles. Presumably the Stuart sisters were holding hands and stretched across him, with two sisters on the right side of his body and the other on the left side. The second photo showed a room neatly stacked with vintage furniture.

As far as anyone could tell, both photos were fakes. Consensus was the creator of the web page had intentionally folded the photos to distort the images, but Aimee noticed the design in the fireplace hearth tiles and realized it matched the tiles in her parlor exactly. Unless the person snuck into the house with friends and spare furniture, how could they have created the image with her fireplace in it?

The web article also stated the sisters were from a long line of European witches and many residents in Port Townsend were witness to their sacrifice of animals and even an infant. It was believed they were trying to cast a youth spell with the blood and sacrifice of their cousin but something went wrong and they all died.

All Aimee could think about was why place the house and land in iron-clad Wills that required everything to remain intact and in the hands of the Stuart family, if the sisters had planned to use black magic to extend their lives? Were they ensuring they had a house to reside in as ghosts; were they the ghosts that everyone is talking about?

Clearing all the documents from the dining room table, Aimee headed up to the third floor to find the boxes she'd packed up from the contents of the house prior to the renovation. She was specifically looking for the Secret Pantry box because she recalled placing hand-written documents and books inside that box, whereas the other boxes contained household items.

As Friday morning dawned, the preparations were nearly complete and the sisters felt confident that they had a sound plan in place, which would withstand all unforeseen circumstances.

"I will go check on Martin and then meet you two in the kitchen," Eliza said as she headed to the guest room.

Martin lay motionless on the bed. Eliza had to lay her head on his chest to verify that his heart was still beating. She wiped his brow and checked his dressings. She knew his life was slipping away and he only had hours to go.

"How is he doing?" Jane asked.

"He is very weak. Let us pray that he survives until tonight," Eliza said. "I think I will sit with him for a while."

With Eliza watching over Martin, Jane and Clair pushed the settee across the foyer and into the dining room and cleared out all the other pieces of furniture. Once the front parlor was empty, Clair retrieved the canister of paint she had purchased from town and carefully painted the outline of a very large pentagram on the hardwood floor.

While they waited for the paint to dry, Clair and Jane collected all the white candles from the storage room plus their parents' Wedding Ring quilt so they could more easily drag Martin into the center of the pentagram.

Present Day ~ Port Townsend

Each time Aimee walked past the calendar hanging on her fridge she saw the letter "M," which she had placed on the date to mark when the ghost or vivid dream first appeared in her bedroom.

For years Aimee had nights where she would wake from her sleep, only to find people standing in her bedroom. They were not frightening to her, just a little intimidating. The individuals generally stood in the doorway, or next to the window, but never moved or tried to talk to her. She had always accepted them as her imagination and tried her best to act like she couldn't see them, just in case they were real and wanted something from her.

Then one night she woke to find an elderly man in the bedroom doorway. He stood there a few seconds and then left the doorway and started moving towards her. Aimee's eyes were locked on him as he moved closer and closer, her right hand fumbling to find the switch to turn on the bedside lamp. The man was only a few feet from her when an elderly woman appeared next to him and grabbed his arm to stop his progression forward. He looked over at her standing there next to him and she shook her head 'no' and then pulled him back to the doorway ;where they both vanished. Needless to say, Aimee could not go back to sleep no matter how exhausted she was. Even with the lights on she was afraid to fall asleep for fear of waking and finding the man standing next to her, almost ready to touch her with his outstretched hand.

After three days of being too afraid to sleep, Aimee found herself in the mental health triage clinic at the local hospital. The following night Aimee was being prepped for a sleep study. Small electrodes were attached to her scalp and lower calves with a red, sticky sap-like substance to monitor her during the night. All of the electrode wires were then plugged into a 6x6-inch box that hung around her neck; eventually the box was connected to the computer monitoring system. Once she was laying on her back in the bed, two very small tubes were placed in her nostrils, along with a third tube which she was instructed to keep snugly between her lips during the night so they could monitor her breathing. Between the fear of rolling over and unplugging the electrodes, or allowing the tube to slide out of her mouth, Aimee was sure she would never fall asleep.

The doctor informed the assistant that he did not want any type of sleep aide used because he wanted a true representation of how Aimee slept. The comment about 'true representation' caused Aimee to laugh. She was pretty sure she did not look like a science experiment when she slept at home.

The results from the study showed Aimee did sleep throughout the entire night, although she personally believed she woke several times and witnessed a woman sitting on the chair next to her bed. Bottom line, according to the doctor, Aimee began to exit REM sleep but was not actually awake. Her brain let her think she was awake, but she was having a vivid dream. The good news was that the nighttime visitors were not real or dead, just extremely realistic dreams. Even with that knowledge, Aimee could not shake

Martin's visit.

****

With the flip of a switch, Aimee brought the Stuart Mansion out of total darkness for the first time in its existence. The mansion lit up the night sky above Port Townsend with the elaborate display of Christmas lights adorning the house and the front yard. As she went from room to room turning on the interior decorations, she sang along with the Christmas music that was playing throughout the house. The fires were lit and the house was glowing with warmth and cheer. By the time she reached the Santa and reindeer display in the foyer, her excitement was just as powerful as when she was a little girl, when her heart grew with anticipation, knowing that her extended family was arriving shortly to spend the holidays with her. Aimee felt truly at peace.

Heading into the kitchen, Aimee took the cold sugar cookie dough from the fridge and began rolling and cutting out all the traditional shapes; her favorite was the Christmas tree. As the cookies baked, the kitchen began to smell sweet and inviting. Once her sister, Pat, and her husband, Jeff, arrived with their three kids, Aimee would seat the kids at the kitchen island and let them decorate cookies until they were so wound up on sugar that they couldn't sit still! Then Aimee, her mom, and sisters could decorate the remaining cookies just like they did when they were children.

The sound of the doorbell told Aimee that her first group of holiday guests had arrived. As she pulled the door open to greet her guests, she herself was greeted by her parents each holding large stacks of gifts. Well, Aimee assumed they were her parents, but wasn't sure until she heard their muffled greetings from behind the gifts.

"Come in," she said, opening the door all the way. "Here, Mom, let me take a few of those for you so you can see where you are going. Dad, if you can hold on a second longer I'll be right back to help you."

"Did you guys leave anything in the stores for other people to buy?" Aimee asked.

"You will know the answer to that question once you help us bring in the rest of the packages! The back seat is full," her dad replied.

"Where did you store these gifts then?" she said, pointing at the ones she had just removed from their hands.

"Oh, they were in the trunk," her mom replied.

"Okay, I know I'm going to regret asking this, but if the trunk was filled with gifts and the back seat is filled with gifts, where is your luggage?"

"Your Dad bought one of those enclosed luggage carriers and mounted it on the roof. Actually, there are a few small gifts in there as well," her mom said.

"You are right, I know the answer to my question: you bought out every store and the rest of Boise will be without presents this year," Aimee said laughingly while she hugged both of her parents.

"So where are Pat and her crew? I thought you were traveling together," Aimee asked, looking outside to see if they had pulled onto the drive.

Frank and Janis Morgan, Aimee's parents, lived in Boise, Idaho. The two families decided to drive to Port Townsend together, but in separate vehicles, once they met-up in Baker City, where Pat and her family lived.

"They stopped downtown so the kids could watch the ferry come into port," Frank said. "They should be here soon."

"I take it you brought the presents and they brought the kids," Aimee stated.

"Oh, no, they have a car full of gifts too," Janis remarked.

"Well, I guess we better move some furniture around in the living room so we can get everything under the tree," Aimee stated.

As Aimee and her parents pushed the furniture back to clear space around the tree, they could hear Pat and her family emerging from their car and the kids running up the stairs to the front door. Aimee raced to the door to greet them, but the minute the door opened, all she received was a tiny tornado of children! All of them were talking at the same time, exclaiming their excitement over seeing the ferry and the enjoyment of spending Christmas at Aunt Aimee's cool house; and on and on they went.

By the time Jeff and Pat reached the door, Aimee was exhausted and wondered how they managed three kids day after day.

"Merry Christmas," Aimee said as she gave them each a hug. "I bet you two are exhausted after that long trip."

"Well, I thought about making the rum balls early and letting the kids eat them, but with my luck they would have become car sick instead of sleeping the entire way," Pat said with a smile. "They were actually pretty good until we reached the Tacoma Bridge and then it was impossible to contain their energy!"

"You are really going to love me then," Aimee said. "I made five dozen sugar cookies for them to decorate and there is enough frosting and candy sprinkles in there to put an elephant into a diabetic coma."

"Well, let's get your things out of the car and then I will give everyone a tour of the famous Stuart Mansion and show you to your rooms," Aimee said.

"Shouldn't we wait for Sarah and Peter?" Janis asked.

"Oh, sorry, Mom; she called just before you arrived to say they wouldn't be here 'til 9AM tomorrow," Aimee replied.

"Aunt Aimee, why is your house famous? Did somebody rich live here, or did a gruesome murder take place here?" Michael, the eldest boy, asked.

"Very close," Aimee started.

"Seriously, people were murdered in this house?" he burst out, not even giving the rich-people option a second thought.

"Let me finish, Michael," Aimee said. "A very rich man from Scotland named Lord William Stuart built this home and lived here with his daughters in the late 1800's."

Aimee thought it best to keep the bit about the murders and possible ghost to herself. She also made Peter and Sarah promise not to say anything. The last thing she wanted were three scared kids, or for that matter, four scared adults.

"That doesn't seem very famous to me," Charlie, the middle boy, replied.

"Perhaps not famous like someone on TV, but in this town, this house is an historical landmark and it is famous," Aimee replied as she ran her hand through the curly red hair on the top of his head.

Once her guests had seen every room and heard all the interesting stories that took place during the renovation, Aimee showed them to their bedrooms.

"What's up those stairs?" Jeff asked.

"Nothing really, it used to be the servants' rooms, but now it's just one large dark, dirty, empty space. I didn't have anything done with it before I moved in. I've thought about putting a theatre room in, or perhaps a home gym. I don't know, I've actually got more space then I can use on the first two floors," Aimee replied.

As Pat rounded up her children, Michael, Charlie and Laurie, and got them settled in the kitchen with cookies and frosting, Aimee opened a bottle of wine and took the tray of hors d' oeuvres she'd prepared earlier into the living room.

"I didn't forget about the three of you," Aimee said when she returned to the kitchen. Opening the fridge she pulled out a tray of sliced fruit, cheese and crackers and placed it on the island.

"If it's okay with your Mom, there's soda in the fridge as well."

As the adults sat in the living room, enjoying the warmth from the fire and the sparkling lights on the Christmas tree, their conversation was periodically interrupted by the sound of Santa saying; 'Merry Christmas -- Are you being good? -- Rudolph and I will be there soon.'

"Is that thing on a timer?" Jeff asked.

"No, it's motion activated. The kids are just having fun," Aimee replied.

At that very moment the Santa went off again and Jeff jumped up from his chair and raced to the foyer to reprimand the kids, but no one was around. He found them laughing and having a good time in the kitchen; decorating the cookies and eating snacks.

"Aimee, I think your Santa has a short or something because the kids are in the kitchen," Jeff said.

"Will you unplug him from the wall, just in case there is an electrical problem? I'd hate to be the one to burn down an historical house that has stood for over a hundred years," Aimee said.

The following morning Pat was busy in the kitchen cooking eggs, sausage and bacon while Aimee whipped up Belgian waffles with strawberry, apple and blueberry toppings. They wanted to have breakfast ready when Sarah and Peter arrived from Seattle.

After breakfast the entire family headed downtown to look at the Christmas decorations and explore the historic town. Aimee knew her mother well enough to know that she wanted to do some last-minute Christmas shopping. The only way her mother could have brought all the gifts she really wanted to bring in their car, would be if she left Dad home and filled his empty seat with presents. Aimee laughed to herself just thinking about her mom's overindulgent love of shopping at Christmas. Several hours, and a multitude of gift bags later, they all returned to Stuart Mansion.

The adults were eager to get inside and sit by a warm fire with a hot drink, but the kids wanted to look around the property, so Aimee agreed to give them a quick tour and, reluctantly, she showed them the cemetery. To her surprise, all three kids found it fascinating and asked a lot of thoughtful questions about the people buried there. Unfortunately, Aimee knew very little about them but promised to call the kids once she did uncover their secrets.

Bursting through the front door, all three kids ran straight into the living room yelling, "There's a cemetery, we saw where dead people are buried, and Aunt Aimee has dead people in her back yard." After calming the kids down, Aimee explained to everyone what they were talking about. Of course, Sarah and Peter already knew about the cemetery and were never concerned by it, nor was Jeff or her dad. However, both Pat and her mom acted like she was off her rocker to buy a place that had an attached cemetery. Worse yet, she kept the graves intact and restored the cemetery.

Aimee reassured her mother and Pat that the residents were no trouble, that they were very quiet and obeyed all the city ordinances. As Aimee expected, they did not find that humorous, but everyone else did.

Pulling Aimee to the side, her mother said, "Why on earth would you show three very impressionable young children a grave yard?"

"First off, it is not a grave yard in a horror movie, it is an historical family cemetery that deserves respect, and the kids found it fascinating, not frightening. They know the people died a very, very long time ago," Aimee said.

Then Pat decided to join the conversation, and as usual, she side with their mother. "How can you live with dead bodies?"

"Pat, they are not in the house; they are several hundred yards away in a garden. You do know that family members were born, got sick and died in these historical houses, don't you? They did not have hospitals or emergency rooms to rush to."

"Yes, of course," Pat said, but they aren't in the house right now and this is going to make the kids hyper all night."

"Well, neither are the Stuarts. They are buried in the back garden and they won't be a problem. Let's just enjoy being together and forget about the former residents. Okay?"

"She's right, Pat," her mother said, "it's ancient history and what's done is done. We will just need to keep a watchful eye on the kids to make sure this discovery doesn't lead to nightmares or day terrors."

"Well, I just don't like it and I think she should have told us about the bodies before we decided to bring our children here. As their mother, it is my duty to protect them from danger and evil people," Pat said angrily.

Aimee knew that both Pat and her mother did not believe in friendly ghosts. However, they did believe in evil spirits and that bad things happen to those who messed with the dead. Sometimes Aimee wondered how she remained sane in her crazy family.

The kids were hyper, but Aimee knew it had nothing to do with the cemetery and everything to do with the sea of presents under the Christmas tree and, of course, Santa's imminent arrival later that evening. As the grandfather clock in the foyer struck 9PM, all three kids raced upstairs.

"What is that all about?" Aimee asked.

"They know that at 9 o'clock they get ready for bed and then come back down to open one present. After that, it's bedtime because no one knows when Santa will arrive and if they are still awake, he won't stop by," Pat said.

No sooner had Pat finished discussing the 9PM ritual, when all three children were back in the living room with their pajamas on.

"Okay guys, you know the drill," their dad said. "Find the three gifts with yellow bows."

Within seconds, each child had a present with a yellow bow in their hands, eagerly tearing the wrappings off.

"Cool, we got flashlights!" Michael said.

"We thought they might be helpful; if you decide to sneak down during the night, at least you will be able to see where you are going," their dad said.

"Say good-night and off to bed," their mother directed.

Christmas morning was always special when Aimee was growing up. The family would wake to the smell of fresh-baked cinnamon rolls and sticky buns. The smell was so powerful that, like an alarm clock, it woke everyone up. They would all head straight to the kitchen where their mother had been for several hours making dough and creating the delicious treats. The rolls and buns that their mother made were so good that the entire family would sit at the table, devouring them and drinking hot chocolate, before they ever went into the living room to see what Santa had left them. Aimee was eager for that experience one more time in her life. Her mother had set out everything she would need prior to going to bed, so she could quietly make the buns and rolls just like she would have done in her own kitchen.

Unfortunately, the sound of Santa's recorded voice wishing a 'Merry Christmas' from the foyer woke Aimee the next morning, not her mother's cinnamon rolls. Quickly going down to turn the Santa off, Aimee discovered that he was not even plugged in. While she stood there trying to figure out if her mind was playing tricks on her again, or if there really was a ghost in the house and he was the one messing with Santa, she realized her mother was in the kitchen working her Christmas magic.

"Merry Christmas, Mom," Aimee said, giving her mom a hug.

"You're up before anything has even gone in the oven. Couldn't you sleep?" her mother asked.

"I thought I heard the Santa talking and came down to shut it off."

"I didn't hear anything, but I have been listening to Christmas music on my new player," she said as she pulled the ear buds out.

"I obviously dreamt it," Aimee said, pouring a cup of coffee. "Can I help you?"

"I take it you are still having trouble with your vivid dreams," her mother commented as she leaned over to give her youngest daughter another hug. "I am sorry."

Within an hour the delicious smell had reached everyone's noses. One by one they came downstairs and arrived in the kitchen eagerly awaiting cinnamon rolls and sticky buns with hot chocolate and coffee. The moment was just as magical as Aimee had remembered it, and she even found herself getting excited to go into the living room to see what was waiting under the tree for her.

"We finally got the last of it out to the trash can area," Jeff said as he walked into the kitchen to pour himself a hot cup of coffee.

"How many black trash bags did you end up using?" Aimee asked.

"Can you believe it? We used twenty!"

"You sure you didn't throw away the presents instead?" Pat asked with a chuckle.

"No, that would have added another hundred bags!"

Aimee was glad to see that her sister had forgotten her anger from the day prior, in regards to the Stuart family. She hoped they could get through the remainder of the visit without any further arguments.

As the little kids and big kids played with their new Christmas toys, the women stayed in the kitchen and prepared a Christmas feast fit for a small kingdom. Not wanting to disappoint anyone, Aimee decided they would make one each of everyone's favorite dish. There would be enough leftovers to feed them for a couple weeks.

Aimee knew that she would be burned out on cooking after the giant Christmas dinner they spent all day preparing, so she hired a catering company from Seattle to provide the buffet and desserts for the New Year's Eve party.

"Alright guys," Aimee said as she entered the living room, "I'm going to need some help so we can be ready for tonight. I need to have the Santa display removed from the foyer and the excess furniture removed from this room."

"Don't worry; honey," her father said, "between Jeff and Peter I'm sure it will be done in no time," he said, giving her a wink.

"When you get that done, there are two air tanks and several bags of balloons that need to be filled."

"Balloons!" Laurie squealed. "I love balloons."

"Yes, sweetie. All of the balloons will be held in a giant net at the top of the ceiling in the foyer. Then at midnight, someone will release them from the net and they will fall down on all of us," Aimee explained.

"Oh, how exciting!" Laurie stated.

"Aunt Aimee, can we help fill the balloons?" Michael asked.

"You will have to talk to those little boys about that," she said as she pointed toward the three men sitting on the sofa playing with Michael's bowling video game.

"So Dad, what do you three call your team, the Geriatric Walker Boys?" Aimee asked.

"Very funny," Peter replied.

"If you win, do you get a lifetime supply of denture cream?" Aimee asked.

In unison, the three men yelled, "Go away," and everyone burst into laughter.

While Pat and Sarah hung streamers and other festive New Year decorations, Janis worked on setting out the dishes that would be used for the buffet. Aimee stayed busy in the kitchen, preparing the strawberries for the Champagne flutes and making her specialty: Marzipan and Cherry Petit Fours.

"So, honey, what else could you use my help with?" her mother asked.

"If you could pour the glaze over the cakes, that would be a huge help," Aimee replied.

"So, how many people did you invite tonight?" Janis asked as she began glazing the cooled cakes.

"Let's see," Aimee said, "I invited Paul Fredrickson, the man who did the renovation on the house, and his wife; Mrs. Conway from City Hall and her husband; the Realtor who sold me the house, Kate; and her husband; and Carol; a friend of mine who works in town and goes to yoga classes with me."

"Sounds like we are going to have a full house tonight," her mother replied.

Rounding up the entire family in the living room, Aimee explained that the string quartet was arriving at 6:30PM to set up their chairs and instruments on the second floor landing and the caterers would arrive by 6:45PM. The guests would start to arrive at 7:30. She then informed them that with only three full bathrooms and seven adults and three children, they were going to need to share. The women were welcome to use the master bathroom, and there was plenty of mirror space in her dressing room for them as well. The men would have to fight it out between the remaining two rooms.

The house was a bustle of activity as everyone put on their formal attire and prepared for a special 1912-themed party. Aimee selected a deep emerald green, full-length gown with an empire waist. She curled her hair and pulled it back on the sides so it draped down the center of her back and showed off her neckline. Her mother selected a dress with a long waistcoat jacket and her sisters each selected chiffon evening gowns. The men wore period appropriate tuxedos.

The guests mingled with each other and moved throughout the house. Aimee tried to spend a little one-on-one time with each guest who she had invited and to give them a personal tour of the house.

Kate's husband was unable to attend and his absence made her feel vulnerable inside the house. Initially, she wandered from room to room rather quickly, always looking more frazzled each time Aimee glanced her way. Eventually she was afraid to move beyond the safety of the foyer. Just in case something happened, she wanted to be close to the exit, Aimee assumed.

Pat took an immediate liking to Kate and she indulged her desire to stay in the foyer. Pat brought her a plate of food and a drink and they made themselves comfortable on the chairs next to the stairs, and chatted about the house. Kate told Pat a variety of stories that she swore were true, even though they had never actually happened to her. She also told her that every time she came into the house she felt as if someone or something was following her around, almost breathing down her neck. A few times she swore that the 'thing' touched her.

"Do you feel anything now?" Pat asked.

"For some reason, this house does not like me and I really don't like being here. I'm also not very comfortable in large crowds, so sitting here is the easiest for me," she replied.

When Kate tried to get Pat to tell her what types of problems Aimee had been experiencing in the house, and Pat stated none that she knew of, Kate got angry and proclaimed no one ever believed her about the house and went away to talk to someone else. However, the conversation had been enough to wake a fear inside Pat and she swore there was something watching her all evening. She told Jeff she couldn't wait to leave the house tomorrow because she knew something was wrong with it.

As midnight drew near, the Champagne flutes with strawberries were passed out to the guests, along with whistles and horns. Everyone moved into the foyer and up the staircase to wait for the grandfather clock to strike 12. They began their countdown on the first strike and on the final gong the band began playing "Auld Lang Syne," the balloons dropped, and everyone yelled, "Happy New Year," while they blew their whistles and horns.

Once everyone had wished and been wished a Happy New Year, they put on their coats and went outside to watch the fireworks display being set off by the Town Council. Stuart Mansion sat in a prime location for such displays and the guests were at eye level for each unique firework as it burst into a rainbow of brilliant colors and spectacular designs.

****

Martin had never, in all his life, seen anything like the Stuart Mansion after Aimee decorated it for Christmas. He just sat in front of each Christmas tree for hours, taking in its beauty and elegant decorations.

The life-size Santa and reindeer in the foyer brought great amusement to Martin. He discovered that with little effort, he could trick the Santa into thinking someone had walked past, and it would turn on and speak its words. Martin was like a little child who could play a joke on others without them knowing he was doing it. So the night Aimee's entire family arrived and everyone was sitting in the living room proved to be too big of a temptation for him. He would wait for the conversation to get going and then he would interrupt them with the words from Santa. Eventually, he realized one of the men was becoming annoyed with his antics and, after the man ran into the foyer looking for the culprit, Martin knew it was time to stop before something happened and Aimee became afraid to live in the house.

Everyone had been asleep for what seemed like ages to Martin, but then the whispers of little kids and the beams of light from their flashlights caught his attention. Following them into the living room, he watched them as they scurried around the tree, trying to see how many presents Santa had left for each of them. Martin could tell it was almost more than they could handle, having to remain quiet and then return to their beds until morning. A large smile appeared on his face and he realized he was actually at peace and happy, something he hadn't experienced in a very long time.

When Aimee's mother got up and went into the kitchen to start her baking, Martin decided to watch her for a while. As he watched, he was taken back to a time when his own mother would get up early to prepare the dough for the daily bread. The rest of the house would be sound asleep, but she would be alone in the kitchen, with only a warm fire to keep her company while she completed her work. Once in a while, Martin would get up and sit with her while she worked and they would talk. He truly missed those moments. Martin thought how his mother would have loved to be working in a kitchen like Aimee's; it would have made her life so much easier, and she happier, because she could have prepared so many dishes in a lot less time.

When Martin tired of watching Janis, he went upstairs to see if Aimee was awake yet. When he found her sound asleep, he decided it was time to wake her so he could spend some time with her before the rest of the family occupied her time. Going back downstairs, Martin attempted several times to make Santa talk, but found it was no longer an easy task. With the determination of a child trying to get what he wanted, Martin focused his energies until Santa spoke. Just as he hoped, Aimee came running down the stairs to quiet the toy. Martin desperately wanted to appear and speak to her, but he was afraid of the problems his presence might cause with her mother and sister; after their outburst the other day over the cemetery.

Following her into the kitchen, Martin sat at the breakfast table and watched Aimee as she helped her mother. He thought Aimee had a beautiful and seductive smile and when she laughed her green eyes sparkled like emeralds in the sun. As he gazed upon her, he knew that she was the one he had been waiting for. Before he knew it, his peaceful moment with Aimee was over and the family was trickling into the kitchen, eager to have something to eat and then open their presents.

Heading back into the living room, Martin sat on the sofa and let the tree lights mesmerize him as he listened to the lively chatter coming from the kitchen.

Once the kids were done in the kitchen, they raced into the living room and began to jump in excitement when they saw, in full light, the mound of presents that Santa had left for them during the night. Their squeals were nearly deafening, but Martin did not mind. He and his brothers and sister never experienced a Christmas morning like this. They may have been joyful for the gift they received, on the years they had extra money and could afford gifts, but they never could have dreamed of waking to a pile of presents like this.

Present after present was handed out to its new owner until there was nothing left under the tree. Then the children's father told them they could start opening their gifts. Bows and paper flew into the air and the process was only interrupted by the periodic yell from each child when they proclaimed that that particular gift was just what they wanted!

Martin wished he could have left a special gift under the tree for Aimee, but there would be no way for her to explain it.

Back to the kitchen the women went, to prepare the Christmas meal. Martin laughed to himself, thinking nothing ever changes. The women perform all the work in the kitchen, and the men sit by the fire and talk. He wondered if that was really how it was everywhere, or was that just how it was with this family?

One drawback to being a ghost is that you cannot smell the food, and Martin desperately wanted to smell the bounty of dishes that were being placed on the dining table. Dish after dish came out from the kitchen, steam rising from most of them, but a few appeared to be cold dishes. His only consolation was that he got to enjoy the experience through the comments of everyone seated around the table. According to the family, the meal smelled amazing and tasted even better. He had to trust them on that, but the fact that everyone filled their plates several times made Martin believe what they said.

The house was fairly quiet for a few days. The children played with their toys, the family spent time together and everyone rested. Then one morning, the calm broke and the house became a bustle of activity again. Within a short time, Martin realized they were preparing for a party and guests from town were going to be attending.

Martin was constantly amazed by Aimee's energy and her ability to make everyone around her happy. His mother would have loved Aimee!

Aimee's father took out his camera and set it up in the foyer, at the bottom of the stairs. He planned to capture everyone as they descended the stairs in the fancy party clothes. Martin eagerly stood next to Frank, waiting for Aimee's turn.

When Aimee arrived at the top of the landing, Martin was frozen in the moment, and everyone else in the house vanished. He believed he was looking at a Princess as she descended the palace stairs and headed into her ball. Her green gown complimented her auburn hair, and she glowed. Martin had never seen a woman as lovely and doubted there was anyone who could compare to Aimee. Her smile lit up her face and her eyes sparkled. Martin knew she was his true love; he could feel it in his soul.

Martin was disappointed when the front door opened and Kate walked into the foyer. He knew Aimee thought well of her, but no matter what he tried he simply did not like her. He followed Kate around the entire night, poking her arm with his finger or breathing down her neck when he simply wanted to see her squirm. Eventually she sat down with Aimee's sister Pat and he stood quietly nearby just listening to their conversation.

When the guests assembled in the foyer, Martin moved to the landing to watch whatever was going to occur. As the balloons dropped and the cheers rang out, he realized they were celebrating what he knew as Scottish Hogmanay. Following everyone outside, he watched Aimee as she watched the fireworks display. By the expressions on her face, he knew she was thrilled with the events of the evening and he was happy for her.

****

Aimee headed up to the third floor to retrieve the box she packed from the Secret Pantry. She recalled placing several books with loose papers inside the box before sealing it. Perhaps they would help her understand the Stuart sisters a little better.

Clearing the table runner and centerpiece from the formal dining table, Aimee laid out the documents Peter provided her and then opened the box and set all the paper material on the table. Sitting at the table Aimee opened a small book that had been lovingly secured with a faded red ribbon. Untying the bow and removing the ribbon, Aimee opened the leather cover and read the first page.

Stuart Family Home - Herb and Flower Beds – Clair Stuart

The next few pages were very detailed drawings of the herb beds, which were located in the backyard directly behind the house. Aimee was impressed at the size of the beds and the quantity of herbs they were capable of producing. Turning the page, Aimee discovered Clair had dried samples of the majority of the herbs and she also wrote a brief description about each herb's use, whether for medicinal or culinary purposes. At the end of the herb section Aimee found another complete section with sketches of the flower beds and then dried samples of the blooms, along with more descriptions and additional notes on those flowers that could be eaten or used to treat an ailment.

Aimee wondered if the sisters practiced some type of holistic medicine. They definitely knew which plants would heal or kill and how to use them. Maybe they were types of midwives, or the village witches, she thought with a laugh.

Setting the journal on the table, Aimee's gaze looked up as she reached in front of her to grab the other book she had retrieved from the box.

"Are you alright?" Martin asked as he watched Aimee, who was sitting motionless. Her right arm remained suspended in midair as she began to reach for the book in front of her.

After a few moments, she laid her arm back on the table and replied, "Well, I know for a fact I am not sleeping, so either you are a ghost or I have just crossed over into crazyville."

"Yes, I am a ghost. I thought we cleared that up a couple nights back," he replied.

"You mean three weeks ago. We did not talk two nights back; it was three weeks ago," she said as she got up from the table and headed into the kitchen, where she immediately returned with the calendar from the fridge.

"See," she said, placing the calendar on the table in front of him. "I wrote the letter 'M' on the day you appeared, and as you can see," she said, flipping the page from December to January, "that was three weeks ago."

Looking up at her, Martin asked, "Why did you put the letter 'M' on the date we spoke?"

"To be honest, I wasn't sure if it was real or a dream and I wanted to track how often it, I mean you, appeared.

"Where have you been all this time?" she asked.

"I was here, thinking."

"Talk about lost in thought," she said. "So you don't have any concept of time, do you?"

"No. If there is no one in the house who lives by a normal routine then I do not notice the difference from day to day."

"But I've been here these past three weeks, living a normal routine."

"I went away to think, and to me it was just a few hours, so I was not paying attention to your routine."

"Okay, how about this: I'll place another letter 'M' on today and as each day passes I will put an 'X' through the day. You just need to look at this to see how much time has passed since our chat today. Don't use my life as your judge of time; I might stay in bed all day and then you wouldn't have a clue as to what day it is."

Pulling out the chair that was next to Martin, Aimee sat down. He looked solid enough, but when she placed her hand on his arm it passed right through. Quickly pulling her hand back and looking into his face she said, "Oh my god, that was weird! Did you sense anything?"

"No. Small things like that don't affect me at all."

Aimee did not spend much time studying his features the first time they met, but now, sitting so close to him, she could see how beautiful his bright blue eyes were and those long brown lashes made them stand out even more. Martin had a strong handsome face and long brown hair which was pulled back into a ponytail and tied off with black ribbon.

"So, is this how you normally dress?" she said, looking at his clothing.

With a chuckle Martin said, "No. I usually wear clothes that fit. I can only assume that this belonged to my Uncle and now it's my funeral suit for all eternity."

"That is a scary thought," Aimee said, "I would hate to find that my family buried me in something that I hated and then I was forced to spend eternity wearing it."

"Can't you take it off?" she asked.

"I've never thought about it," he said. "I don't have anything else to wear if I don't wear this."

"Well, I didn't mean for you to run around naked, but I was thinking that removing the jacket might give you a better look."

Martin stood and removed the jacket, laying it across the back of the chair; it immediately vanished once his hand let go of it.

"Where did it go?" Aimee asked.

"I do not know; I have never taken it off before," he replied with bewilderment.

"I think it's safe to assume that your clothes only remain visible and tangible when they are on you physically. Once you let go of that jacket, it vanished," she said.

As Martin stood there Aimee could tell there was something bulky under his dress shirt.

"Martin, will you take your shirt off too, please," she said, and then looked at him in horror.

"Wow, did that sound as bad to you as it did to me?" she asked. "What I meant was: There is something bulky under the shirt. What is it?"

Once Martin stopped laughing at how flustered Aimee had become over her comment, he looked down and realized she was right. There was something strange under his shirt.

As he removed the shirt and began to place it on the back of the chair Aimee yelled, "Stop. Don't let go of the shirt or it will vanish too. Just hold on to it."

As he stood there, holding his shirt, they both realized what it was on his stomach; it was the gauze bandages that had covered his wounds. With his free hand Martin tried removing it, but was unable.

"I've got an idea, tie the shirt around your waist and then you will be able to use both hands to remove the bandages," Aimee suggested.

Once Martin had removed the bandages, he dropped them on the floor and they vanished just like the jacket. Aimee could see where there were four long gashes in his stomach and side. She could also see how physically fit he had been during his life. His chest muscles were well defined and his biceps were large. This was the body of a man who did not sit around watching TV and playing video games; he spent his life doing strenuous manual labor and it showed in his strong physique.

All Aimee could think about was how gorgeous the dead man in her dining room was. "Get a grip on reality," she mentally told herself. "Okay, well, how about you put the shirt back on," she said as she quickly left the room and headed into the kitchen.

"Is everything alright?" Martin asked as he entered the kitchen.

"Oh yes, fine. I just wanted to make some coffee," she said, quickly turning on the faucet and grabbing the pot.

"You should roll the sleeves up so you look more relaxed," she said, keeping her focus on the act of making coffee.

When Aimee did look up she discovered Martin was no longer standing in the kitchen. "Martin, where did you go?" she asked aloud, thinking he had vanished again.

"I'm in here," he replied, "looking at the papers you have on the table."

With a sense of relief that he had not vanished again, Aimee went back into the dining room.

"So, what have you got here? Have you learned anything?" Martin asked.

Aimee showed Martin the newspaper clippings and the images of the crime scene from the internet. She explained that all she really knew was that four people had died in her living room. The why, and how, were still a mystery but she was beginning to research the information she found in the house and hoped it would shed more light on the sisters, and help her piece together what their motive was and what actually happened.

"What have you learned about the sisters?" he asked.

"Not a lot; I've just started. I found Clair's 'Herb and Flower Journal.' She documented everything she grew and she even sketched designs of each garden bed.

"Does that tell you anything about Clair?" he asked.

"I would say she was very detail-oriented, loved to garden and was extremely knowledgeable about the healing qualities of plants in general."

"That's not uncommon," he said. "Every village or community would have at least one person who knew how to use nature to heal the sick."

"Before you start looking through the other books could you place all the documents in that pile out on the table so I can read them?" he asked as he pointed to the stack of documents Peter had presented her with.

"Sure, no problem. Just let me know if you need something turned over to read the back."

As she spread out the files, she asked, "Are you unable to touch anything in my world?"

"Not exactly. I can pass through objects such as doors, walls and furniture. I can also make things move short distances. It requires a lot of energy and it leaves me drained for long periods of time so I don't do it very often."

"Well, just let me know if you need assistance. Having another person's thoughts about this whole situation will be of great help to me."

After getting a cup of coffee, Aimee settled back into her chair and began looking at the second book she had retrieved from the box. This one turned out to provide insight into Jane.

Aimee found a collection of recipes that had been lovingly written on individual sheets of paper and secured in a leather cover. From this Aimee was able to learn that Jane loved to cook and bake and that she took great pride in her recipe collection. She found several recipes that had special notes written on them. One said

'Father's Favorite' and another indicated that Clair recommended using lavender to add a flavorful surprise. Aimee was eager to try some of Jane's recipes so she decided to place the collection with her own cookbooks.

When Aimee returned from the kitchen, she realized Martin was no longer at the table but had gone into the living room. He was standing as close to the center of where the pentagram had been as he possibly could, without standing inside the large ottoman.

"Did you remember something?" she asked.

"I'm not sure, but the crime-scene picture you showed me, was taken in this room and I'm pretty sure it's me on the floor."

"Does anything else seem familiar?" she asked.

"The message that they found pinned to the walls; that is something I do remember."

"What does it mean?"

"I remember it; I didn't say I understood it," he said, turning around to look at Aimee.

"Alright, what do you remember about it?"

"I don't know how long I had been a ghost, or how many people I had frightened away, but one day I heard two men in this room, talking about the message and it came back to me. The sisters had repeated it over and over to me. I don't know why, or what they expected me to do with the information."

"Did you stop scaring women away after you remembered the message?" she asked as they walked back to the dining table.

"I eventually scared them away, once I knew they couldn't be my true love."

"So, you are saying I'm your true love and that's why you have allowed me to stay?"

"I haven't decided yet," he said, giving her a wink.

"Maybe you were to guard the house until the right person came along, and then she gets to decide if you can stay," she replied with smile.

"Well, I don't know about you, but this has been a long and very strange day. I think I'm going to call it quits, order a pizza and watch a little TV," Aimee said. "You're welcome to watch TV with me if you would like."

"Yes, I would. Will you be watching the show about the man who travels to strange places in a blue box?"

Aimee burst out laughing. For all the things for a ghost to want to watch, "Sure, we can watch that."

"Aimee, is that show and the other one you watch, the one with the brothers who are vampires, are they real?"

"No. Well, now that I've met you I'm not sure, but I'll stick with no. They are just stories someone created, perhaps based on a story they heard once or just ideas from their wild imagination."

"So nothing is true?"

"Well, I wouldn't say that. Most are stories to entertain you, but a few are based on incidents that actually happened. Like war movies; the story line or plot is made up for the most part, but the war and how bad it was, that is generally depicted as realistically as possible."

****

As the first glimmer of dawn forced its way through the winter sky, and she began to wake up, Aimee was surprised at how well she slept during the night. As she lay there, she started mentally running through yesterday's events and she realized why she had slept so well: Martin was not a vivid dream but a real ghost. She was not going crazy.

A blast of wind slammed against the side of the house and Aimee could hear the lavender wreath being pulled from her bedroom window. Looking towards the window she realized Martin was sitting in the wing chair, gazing out towards the bay.

"Been there long?" she asked.

"Actually, I do not know how long I've been sitting here watching the storm roll in. I came in to see if you were awake but found you sleeping, so I just sat down. Time gets lost when you have an eternity of it."

"So, do I snore?" she asked with a laugh.

"To be honest, I don't think you ever moved or made any sounds."

"Well, it sounds like a bad storm has landed. I need to call Landscapes by Design and tell them to postpone taking down the lights and wreaths. I would hate for someone to get hurt by being on a ladder in this wind," she said, reaching for her phone.

"Probably a good idea; one ghost per house is enough," he said with a chuckle.

"No kidding. The last thing I want is to run a boarding house for the dead."

"It dawned on me when I woke this morning that we have heard from Clair with her garden journals and we have heard from Jane with her collection of cherished recipes, but we have not heard from Eliza. There was nothing of hers in the Secret Pantry, and all of the other items I collected from the other rooms were pretty random; nothing specific to one person."

"You're right; and as the eldest, I cannot imagine she would not leave something of herself behind. Perhaps we missed it and it was tucked in with Jane and Clair's notes."

"Possible, but I have a feeling she would have left something significant. Perhaps an explanation of what happened to the four of you and how your true love is supposed to set you free. I don't know, but I'm sure she left something major."

"Aimee, what if she did leave it and someone over the years has removed it from the house? What do we do then?"

"With you on guard all those years I doubt most of the tenants had enough time to snoop through the cupboards and closets before you scared them off. In fact, I bet most of them left their things behind in their hurry to leave!" she said with a laugh.

"Then where is it?" he asked.

"Tell you what. You go wait for me in the dining room. Once I get dressed I'll be down and we can take one more look through the documents. Then I will go upstairs and open each one of those boxes and go through the contents. Who knows how she left her message."

Although Aimee could no longer see Martin sitting in the chair, she wondered if he was still there, just invisible. Then again, what did it matter if he could see her; he was just a ghost.

When Aimee entered the dining room Martin was sitting at the table waiting for her. "Let me put the coffee on and then I'll spread everything out again," she said, heading straight into the kitchen. When she rounded the corner, she found Martin standing next to the coffee pot.

"Wow, you really can move through walls because you did not walk past me."

"Yes, it makes moving from one room to another quicker and more effective, especially when you want to frighten someone. When they run from the room screaming and into another room, all I have to do is quickly float through the walls and I'm there waiting for them. That frightens them even more."

"Thanks, I'll remember that," she said.

"Do you believe my cousins were witches?" Martin asked.

"Well, in a way, yes. I think they knew how to use herbs and plants to heal the sick, or possibly kill. I think they were in tune with Mother Nature and perhaps they were born with special gifts."

"I'm sorry, but I don't understand what 'special gifts' they could have been born with," Martin stated.

"There are people in the world today who claim they can see the dead," she said and then started laughing, "and now, I guess I am one of those people."

"Anyhow," she continued, "others have the ability to know what is going to happen in the future and some can read minds. I don't know how much I believe, but then again I didn't really believe in ghosts. So yes, the sisters could have been psychic or clairvoyant or maybe real witches. There is so much in this world that we do not understand."

After careful re-examination of all the documents from the Secret Pantry, Aimee and Martin climbed the stairs to the third floor and Aimee began opening each box and pulling out its contents. Once they were sure a message from Eliza was not hidden in the items, she placed them back in the boxes. After several hours they had completed their search, but still had not found a message from Eliza.

"I'm starving, let's go into town and get fish and chips," Aimee said, looking over to Martin and they both started laughing.

"Okay, how about I go into town for fish and chips and you think about this house and where there might be another hidden panel or secret room like we found in the pantry. The restoration crew did not tear out every single wall and floor board so we still might find something. You definitely know this house better than anyone."

"I'll do my best," he replied.

Just as Aimee was about to open the front door to leave, she turned around and called out.

"Martin, when you walk through walls, can you see inside the walls? Or do you have to close your eyes?"

"No, I can see, but the space between the walls is very narrow so there is not much to look at."

"Perhaps while I'm gone, you can start walking through the full length of each wall in every room and see if there is anything hidden between the walls," she said.

****

As Aimee waited for her dinner at the Captain's Table Family Restaurant, she stared out the window and watched the ferry bringing passengers across from Seattle. Her thoughts were weighing heavily on her mind and the steady movement of the ferry was lulling her into a state of self-hypnosis. If she wanted to hide something in the house, something that she did not want anyone to find by chance, where would she hide it? The Secret Pantry was obviously a hiding place, but too easily discovered. The items she found in there were highly interesting, but nothing that explained what she needed to know. The only hope was that Martin could find something hidden between the walls.

When Carol, the waitress, placed Aimee's order in front of her, she did not respond. Carol then placed her hand on Aimee's shoulder to see if everything was okay. Aimee jumped in her seat and turned around to face Carol. Placing her hand over her chest, Aimee said, "Oh my god, you scared me!"

"Aimee, are you okay?" Carol asked.

"Oh, sorry Carol, I was just lost in thought."

"I'm sorry. I didn't mean to scare you. Is there something going on at the Stuart place? You seem really nervous. "

"Oh no, nothing like that," Aimee quickly replied. "I was just zoning and wondering how the passengers on the ferry could stand to cross in such bad weather. Personally, I dread making that crossing even on the best of days."

Aimee slowly made progress on consuming her meal because her mind was so focused on the search going on at her home, by a ghost. When Carol returned the first few times, Aimee was sitting there staring out the window. Just before her third return to the table, Carol glanced over and noticed that Aimee had pushed the plate away from herself. Carol brought the check and placed a small to-go box on the table, telling Aimee it was a piece of double chocolate cake, guaranteed to make everything look brighter. Aimee thanked her and returned to Stuart Mansion.

****

"Martin, I'm back," Aimee said as she closed the front door behind her and placed her coat on the bench. Turning around she found Martin sitting on the fourth step of the staircase.

"Any luck?" she asked.

"I'm sorry, but nothing. I've completed the entire first floor and the only thing I discovered was a large empty space under the stairs that you could possibly use as a storage area if you had a panel door installed."

Laughing out loud Aimee said, "You could actually earn a living, online giving remodeling tips. You would never have to leave the house and they wouldn't know you were a ghost."

"I'll keep that in mind should you start charging me room and board," he replied.

"Well, hopefully the next floor will prove our theory," she said, heading up the stairs with Martin following close behind.

Once she reached the landing and turned towards her bedroom, she stopped and turned to Martin, "You are free to search the other side of this floor, but my bedroom area is off limits for now. I'm going to soak in the tub and then get in bed and read a book and eat this chocolate cake," she said, holding up the to-go box.

Martin agreed and headed in the other direction. Aimee thought he looked disappointed when she told him she wanted private time and that he would not be able to spend the evening with her, and she began to feel bad. Martin had helped her all day and she had left him alone while she went into town to eat, and then as soon as she returned home she sent him away. He may be a ghost, but Aimee knew her actions were not the way you treat a friend, dead or alive.

The following morning when Aimee woke she discovered Martin laying on the bed next to her, propped up on his elbow just watching her.

"Talk about waiting an eternity," he said. "Feels like I have been here forever waiting for you to wake up."

"You could have done something to wake me."

"No, I didn't want to frighten you; besides, you looked so lovely and peaceful being asleep I just decided to wait."

"Okay, I'm awake, and you are acting like a little kid who just discovered where his parents hid his birthday presents."

"I did discover something," he said with enthusiasm.

"What?!" Aimee asked, sitting up in bed with real intrigue.

"Oh, maybe I shouldn't tell you. How do I know you are the one I've been waiting for?" he said with a sly grin.

Quickly pulling the bed pillow from behind her, Aimee swung it at Martin, forgetting he was a ghost until the pillow lay on the opposite side of the bed, and Martin sat unaffected.

"Now, that's just not fair," she said. "I can't even get back at you!"

"Well, I guess I'd better tell you then," he replied.

"I waited until you were asleep and then I searched the second floor. I did find some papers rolled up and tucked under the floor board in one of the guest bedrooms."

Jumping out of bed, Aimee nearly fell on her face when her foot got tangled in the blankets. Martin was immediately in front of her, to catch her if he actually could have; but she caught her balance just in time. Aimee found Martin's gesture sweet.

"Come on; show me where you found the papers."

Martin led Aimee into the guest bedroom that was opposite the landing from her bedroom. She turned on the light and went over to the board where Martin was pointing. Aimee knelt down and pushed on the ends of the board, but nothing happened.

"You're sure there is something under here?" she said.

Kneeling down next to her, Martin leaned over and stuck his head through the hardwood floor.

"Yes, there are papers in here," he said as he removed his head from inside the floor and looked at Aimee with a grin.

"That is just wrong on so many levels," she said, staring at him.

Martin just burst into a deep robust laugh.

"Fine, you sit here laughing by yourself and I'll go get a hammer and screwdriver to pry that board up."

When Aimee returned Martin was still happy with his little prank. Aimee wished she could find a way to get even, but how do you prank a ghost?

"Here's hoping I don't cause the entire house to collapse. This could be a trap."

"What do you mean?" Martin asked.

"Well, if I don't open this up in the exact way the owner closed it, I might cause a series of events that would force the house to collapse in order to protect their secret," she said as she positioned the screwdriver in the crack between the boards and raised the hammer to strike a blow.

"Stop!" Martin yelled as he attempted to grab her hand.

This time it was Aimee's turn to burst out laughing. She hadn't intended him to take her seriously, but realized you can prank a ghost.

"What's so funny?" Martin asked.

"You," she replied. "I made that stuff up because that's what happens in the movies and you fell for it. Now we are even," she said, swinging the hammer down, making contact with the handle of the screwdriver. The board moved a little.

With a few more strong hits the board popped loose from its resting place. Sliding the screwdriver under the board Aimee lifted it up to reveal what looked like an old scroll tied with black ribbon. Carefully removing the papers she stood and headed out of the room.

"Where are you going?" Martin asked.

"Oh, sorry, to the kitchen; that room has the brightest lights and I want to look at these. Plus, I need some coffee."

"You would think this world couldn't function without coffee," he replied.

"Trust me, it can't!"

Aimee sat at the kitchen island and untied the ribbon. As she unrolled the papers, she realized they were very old and proceeded with great care. Carefully laying each of the pages on the counter and holding the corners down with cups she discovered she was looking at magic spells.

"What do you make of those?" she asked Martin as she poured herself a cup of coffee.

"Some kind of black magic, and I'm sure you don't want to mess with these," he said.

"I wasn't planning on performing them, but we need to be sure they aren't a clue from Eliza."

"Well, maybe the other items I found will help you determine if these are important."

"What other items? You didn't say you found more things, just these."

"Actually, you never gave me a chance. Once I told you about the papers you were racing to get out of the bed and find them. I figured we would do one thing at a time."

"Okay, we're done with this thing. What else did you find?" she said eagerly.

"On the third floor," he began.

"There's nothing up there but a large empty room covered in years of dust and spider webs," Aimee interjected.

"Actually, there is something up there. I just forgot about it."

"And what was that?"

"That I took over a man; I got inside of him."

"WOW, how do you forget something like that?" she asked

"Long before you arrived here, there was a man who constantly poked around the third floor. He didn't have a key to unlock the door, but I knew he wanted inside the room. One day when he arrived with tools to take the door down, I decided I needed to enter his body and possess him long enough to have him construct a full-length wall. He ordered the construction supplies and they were delivered a few days later."

"How long did you stay in him?"

"Long enough to get the wall built, but probably too long for him. Within a few days of me leaving him, he became dangerously confused and eventually the town's people had him taken away before he harmed himself, or someone else. Once he was gone, I retired inside the locked room where I laid on the floor until I regained my energy, safe in the knowledge that no one would find the room now."

"What's inside the locked room?"

"The room itself is the children's nursery and the only things in there are books and toys. But there's also a hidden room. I don't know how to open it and last night was the first time I've ever been inside it," he said.

"So, what did you see in there?" Aimee asked impatiently.

"There are candles and jars and items that I would say were used in the practice of black magic. There's also a very large bundle wrapped in cloth, a small satchel and an envelope sitting on top. The envelope says, 'For Martin's True Love'."

"That must be what Eliza left behind! We have to get into that room," Aimee said racing out of the kitchen and up the stairs. Stopping half way, she turned around and walked back into the kitchen.

"Forget your coffee?" Martin asked.

"Very funny, but no. The third floor doesn't have electricity and it is really dark up there. Plus, it's really dirty and scary."

"There's nothing scary up there; remember, 'I'm the scary ghost'."

"Actually, I was thinking more on the lines of spiders. Besides, I need something to break through the false wall you had built and some type of light to see what I'm doing."

"What do you propose?" Martin asked.

"A trip to Home-Savers where I can get some supplies; but first, I think I'll get dressed."

When Aimee returned from her shopping trip, she packed in six bags of long extension cords so there would be several hundred feet to run electricity from the second floor to the flood lamps she purchased to brighten the dark space. In addition she purchased a small electric saw, goggles, gloves and a sledge hammer. That wall was going down and she did not care what kind of damage she inflicted upon it during the process.

As Aimee carried the bags to the second-floor landing and began connecting the extension cords, she filled Martin in on her thoughts. She believed the nursery was the first half of the message, *'Guard the children's memories'* and that; for whatever reason; was why he was drawn to the nursery as his home in death. It also explained why he felt compelled to possess Paul the head of the restoration crew, to keep him from getting into the room. If she wasn't the true love he was waiting for, then the book would be discovered and removed before Martin could be set free.

Once the lights were in place and Aimee could see what she was up against; she carried the rest of the gear upstairs.

"What are you going to do?" Martin asked.

"I'm going to knock out a section of that wall so I can reach through and unlock the door and enter the nursery. Yes, I know that sounds easy enough, but trust me, you don't want to watch me do this. It will be painful and embarrassing and not something I want another living, or dead, person to witness."

With a sweep of her hand she banished Martin from the third floor. He walked out of the room like a gentleman, but then being a ghost and very intrigued by this woman; he became invisible and returned to watch.

With each impact of the hammer against the wall; he could see how difficult it was for her to gather the strength to take the next swing. She stopped several times to catch her breath and shake out her arms, but went right back to pounding the wall. Little by little, she began to cause damage and, once she had punched a hole through the outside layer, she turned on the saw and started to cut the wall and the boards. Several hours passed before she went downstairs.

"Martin, where are you?" she called out.

"In the kitchen," he replied.

Aimee found him sitting patiently at the center island, looking at the papers she had placed there earlier.

"I'm done. I can unlock the door and go inside," she said, taking off her gloves and laying them on the counter.

The palms of her hands were raw and bleeding. "I'm not used to hard labor," she said, sitting next to him and looking at the sores.

Martin leaned over, kissed his fingers and made the gesture of laying them on her hands. "You are remarkable, Aimee."

"Thanks," she said with a tired smile, "I can't feel my arms they are so weak. I think I'm going to soak in the tub and go to bed. The room will still be there tomorrow," she said, "especially with you guarding it."

April 1872 ~ Port Townsend

Nearly two years had passed since Henry and Martin were separated by the crew of the Windspur, making Henry's return to Port Townsend even more important to him than it was to the other members of the crew. Henry had overheard the men who grabbed him that night on the beach talking about stabbing the other guy and leaving him for dead. Henry was determined to find out what really did happen to Martin that night.

The relentless gossip surrounding the witches and sacrifice had died down after the first year, but unfounded fears of demons and ghosts had forever cast a shadow of gloom over the Stuart Mansion. It did not take Henry long to learn of the gruesome deaths of three sisters and their male cousin. Although he wanted to believe Martin had survived and was married, with a child on the way, living the life of a farmer, the feeling in the pit of his stomach told him that his best friend, his brother, was dead.

Taking leave of his shipmates as they got drunk and squandered away their pay, Henry headed out to the Stuart Mansion to pay his final respects to his beloved friend. So many thoughts raced through his mind as he progressed on his journey, the same path Martin would have taken two years earlier. What would have happened if they both had arrived at the Stuart Mansion, would the sisters have killed both of them? Or would they have been forced to kill the sisters in order to save their own lives? He just couldn't imagine the fear that Martin must have experienced when he realized his own cousins, his family, were about to sacrifice him for some evil purpose.

The cemetery had not been cared for since the bodies had been laid to rest. The weeds were nearly the height of the head stones and it made it difficult to see where to walk with respect for the dead. Henry knelt down by each headstone and cleared away the debris, reading the name of each deceased person. But he did not see one for Martin. For a brief moment, Henry's heart jumped with joy and excitement, thinking that he had been wrong and Martin was not the male cousin who was sacrificed.

As he stood and stepped away from the fourth headstone, he realized his foot had landed on something hard. Not the ground, but a flat surface. Kneeling back down, Henry cleared away the neglected growth and realized his worst nightmare was real. The stone read: *Our Loving Cousin – Corporal Martin Samuel Stuart – May 1870.*

Henry felt as if a powerful gale had slammed him across his back, knocking the breath out of his lungs. He knelt there, bracing his hand on the stone, starrng at Martin's name, not even realizing that tears were streaming down his face and falling on the grave. Henry had never experienced such a great loss in his life and prayed he would never feel this way again, because it was unbearable.

Henry assured Martin that he was happy and safe and promised to live his life for the both of them.

****

Martin's thoughts were fuzzy as he woke; he thought he heard Henry speaking to him as he opened his eyes, only to find himself alone in a dark room. Allowing his eyes to adjust to the darkness, he realized he was in a children's nursery. How he got there or why he was there was unclear to him. The last solid memory that he had was of he and Henry leaving the saloon and heading to the Stuart Mansion. Martin felt like it had been a very long time since he thought of Henry and that saddened him because Henry would never give up on Martin and would search for him, because that is what best friends do.

Once Martin's eyes acclimated to the dim light in the room, he located the door and reached for the door knob, only to discover that his hand passed right through it. Time and time again he reached for the knob and each time was unable to grasp it. In frustration Martin slammed his fists against the door and found himself lying on the floor in a hallway, on the opposite side of the nursery room door. Getting to his feet, he followed the hallway to the stairs and descended to the foyer on the first floor.

The house seemed vaguely familiar but completely strange at the same time. By the look of the dust on the furniture, and the cobwebs, the house had not been lived in for a very long time. Wandering from room to room, Martin tried to piece together his thoughts from the last moment he saw Henry to the moment he awoke, upstairs in the nursery, but no thoughts or images would solidify in his mind.

Martin could tell time was passing when night turned into day and day into night, but he did not know how much time had passed or how much time was currently passing. The only thing he was sure of was the fact that he was a ghost, lost and very angry.

Present Day ~ Port Townsend

Aimee knew exactly where to find the key to unlock the nursery. She had packed away a ring of keys that she found in the Secret Pantry. When she opened the box; she decided to hang the keys in the main foyer as a piece of décor. Retrieving the keys from the center of the picture frame she showcased them in, she then headed to the top floor. As usual, the key that finally fit the lock was the last one she tried. Butterflies swirled in her stomach as she heard the lock move and turned the handle to open the door.

As Aimee entered the nursery she saw Martin standing near the fireplace with a smug look on his face.

"Oh, you are funny," she said, "My body aches from tearing down a wall to get in here and you just walk through the wall."

"Death has its perks," he said, laughing.

"Where is the secret room?" she asked.

"Behind the wall, to the right of the fireplace; I can see a lever on the inside to release the latch and open the panel, but I do not know where the mechanism is hidden that releases the lever and latch."

"It has to be on or in the fireplace," she replied.

"Why do you assume that?"

"Because in the movies that is where the lever is always hidden, and once they touch it, the secret panel opens. The only problem, it is too dark in here to see what I'm touching so I will need to bring in the lights."

Aimee combined the two extension cords in order to have enough cord length to bring the light into the nursery. Setting it directly in front of the fireplace, she knelt down and began pressing each brick inside the hearth. One by one and row by row she pressed every inch of each brick until she was finally to the last brick, and still she had not discovered the button's hiding place.

As she stood, Martin asked, "Now what?"

"Now, I start at the bottom-left corner of the mantel and I press every single inch of it until I have made my way to the bottom-right corner," she replied as she moved into position to begin on the mantel.

Martin had never met anyone like her before. She was beautiful, funny, intelligent, very loving and, most of all, determined. This was a woman who knew what she wanted and was not going to stop until she had it. Most people would have given up early on, in the quest to figure out the mystery, but not Aimee. She was willing to suffer physical pain and exhaustion to help someone she didn't even know.

"Martin, Martin," she yelled as she stood with her hand pressed on the third thistle down on the right side of the mantel. Her head turned to the right and she looked at the panel that had just popped open.

Releasing her pressure on the mechanism she took a step towards the panel and, as she passed Martin, she punched him in the arm, saying, "Snap out of it!"

The movement of her hand and arm passing through his spiritual energy made them both jump. "I don't care how many times that happens, it still freaks me out," Aimee stated.

"Now that you are back from your daydream, look at what I found," she said as she pushed the panel the remainder of the way open.

Turning the light to face the entrance to the secret room, Aimee stepped inside. "This is so exciting!" she said as she slowly walked around the small space.

"I can just imagine how Howard Carter must have felt the first time he stepped inside King Tut's tomb. Both rooms were hidden and meant to remain so, but both rooms were eventually discovered, and everything within them was just as it had been when the last person left and sealed their entrances."

"You are amazing, Aimee. You see everything with such enthusiasm that I actually feel alive just being around you," Martin said.

Looking into his eyes and smiling, Aimee said, "You are pretty special yourself, and that is why I want to help you."

Aimee gathered the stack of items that rested underneath the note for 'Martin's True Love' and headed down to the dining room to see what Eliza had to tell them.

****

"Sit next to me," Aimee suggested as she pulled the chair out from the table, "then we can look at it together. We will be the first eyes to look upon it since Eliza locked it away."

Opening the envelope, Aimee removed a letter which Eliza had written:

My Dearest Child,

My sisters and I believe we did everything we could to ensure Martin's wait was only a few years at most. I pray that you arrived quickly.

You must have a thousand questions to ask, but I will only be able to tell you what you need to know, which is how to complete the spell and bring Martin back to life.

Aimee stopped reading and just stared at the words, 'bring Martin back to life.' Looking over to Martin she said, "Are they serious? I thought they wanted me to set your spirit free to cross over to the other side."

"You do not wish for me to be alive?" Martin asked.

Aimee could see the hurt in his eyes. "Oh god no, Martin, that is not what I meant at all! If my role is to do that for you, then I will. It just sounds a bit scary, as far as magic goes. We both know how their last big spell ended."

You will find all of the tools you need in the roo, inside our nursery, where you found this letter. The herbs you will require can be found behind a hidden panel in the kitchen pantry. You will need to move all the crates we stacked in front of the wall to see the handle. Finally, there is a scroll hidden in Clair's room. It is under the floor board in the far left corner of the room.

We gave our lives as penance for a sin our Mother performed against nature. We have never performed the dark arts, but stayed true to the healing power of Mother Nature. This will be our first and last deviant from our true belief. Believe me when I say, we do not undertake this task lightly.

Our Cousin has much to live for and we have the power to change his fate with the aid of our Mother's dark magic. The evil our Mother unleashed in Scotland still affects those residing there, but it will take someone with greater power than ours to return it to the evil place from which it was born. However, our selfless sacrifice will keep it from taking permanent hold in this world.

You will find the instructions to perform the ritual on the page marked with the white ribbon in our book of spells. The spell we will cast on Friday night can only be broken for the duration of one full moon. Therefore, we are each sacrificing our life to offer Martin three lunar cycles. You must truly love each other for this to work, because true love is the strongest magic in the world and true love will compensate for your lack of natural magical abilities.

I cannot leave you, with a clear conscience if I do not tell you: the use of dark magic always requires payment and you cannot cheat on that payment.
God Bless You,
Eliza, Jane and Clair Stuart

"What the hell did she mean, it will require a payment?!" Aimee blurted out, looking at Martin.

"She meant that I cannot stay alive for more than the three lunar cycles. We cannot escape what is meant to be, my ultimate death."

With shaking hands, Aimee returned the letter to the envelope and placed it on the table, stating, "Let's see what else she left us."

Removing the items sitting on top of the spell book, Aimee unwrapped the covering that had been protecting the book for over 100 years, a bit longer than the sisters had planned, Aimee thought to herself. Locating the white ribbon, Aimee opened the book to the selected pages.

The page on the right-hand side was a magical spell to create an Amulet Bag for protection. It listed all the herbs required and how they were to be placed in the bag.

"Aimee, didn't you destroy all of the jars from their Secret Pantry?" Martin asked.

"I did, but they wouldn't have been any good after all of these years. I can purchase all of these from an online herb grower. No problem here," she replied with a big smile.

The left side of the book contained more written instructions from Eliza:

This book only contains spells for white magic. We could not store the dark art spells here, so they are hidden in

*Clair's room. Keep this spell book separate from the dark
art spells, but do not worry about other hidden spells, as we
have destroyed everything.*

*You will require the use of a dagger, one that has
belonged to a witch. Our personal daggers will be used and
lost once we perform the ceremony on Friday night. You will
find our Mother's dagger, wrapped in cloth, among the
contents I set aside for you. Clair hid the dagger in a stuffed
bear and we brought it from Scotland with our books and
toys. You will need our Mother's power.*

"Oh, Lord, I'm feeling sick," Aimee said as she stopped
reading. "A dagger, they want me to use a dagger. That seriously
sounds like something is going to end badly."

"Breathe, Aimee, don't panic until you have read
everything," Martin said.

"You're right. Why panic a bit at a time? I'll read
everything and then have a nervous breakdown."

*For any love spell to work, there must be physical
items that belonged to the missing lover. We placed all of
Martin's personal belongings in the brown leather bag and
have selected the locket as the primary item.*

*Inside the locket you will find locks of hair from
Martin, Jane, Clair and myself; you will add a drop of your
blood when the time is right.*

All ritual spells require a pentagram and you will find everything you need to know in this book. Look for the yellow ribbon.

Finally, we performed the original ceremony at the first full moon in May. You will add great strength to your spell if you do it at midnight leading into the same full moon. I wish I could tell you what will happen, but we have never performed these spells.

"Okay, a drop of blood does not sound too bad, right Martin?" Aimee questioned as she looked over to Martin.

He was no longer paying attention. She followed his gaze to the brown leather bag sitting on the table.

"Aimee, will you open that please?" he asked.

"Sure, sweetie, no problem," she said as she reached for the bag and loosened the draw strings.

The first thing she pulled from the bag was a smaller bag. Opening the draw strings, she poured the contents into her hand. There were ten gold coins. Setting those on the table, she reached into the larger bag and removed a very old letter addressed to Lord William Stuart on one side and sealed with red wax on the other side. The final items to emerge from the bag were the locket and a gold ring with a large ruby. Aimee sat the items in a straight line in front of Martin and left him alone to look at them.

When Aimee returned to the dining room, she did not find Martin sitting at the table. She found him in the living room, looking at the floor.

"Martin, are you okay?" she asked.

"As good as a dead man can be," he replied and headed back to the dining table.

"How does one's life end up like this? Henry and I came here to start over," he said, pointing to the letter of introduction his father had provided, "and he is abducted and I'm turned into a ghost by my own family."

"I cannot imagine what you are going through, Martin," Aimee offered. "I can only believe that the Universe has bigger plans for you than simply living and dying in the 1800's."

"Do you recognize the other items?" she asked.

"Yes. My father's Solicitor presented them to me after I returned from the War. The coins were all that was left from my father's estate and the locket was a gift to my mother when they were courting. The ring was her wedding ring, and she wanted one of her boys to present it to his future wife."

With that said, Martin vanished. Aimee did not look for him immediately; she wanted to allow him time to process what had happened and what was going to happen. Or maybe she just wanted to have time to process the information herself. Either way, she let him be.

Present Day ~ Port Townsend

Although the Stuart sisters had pushed the furniture from their front parlor into the dining room and then painted a massive pentagram on the parlor floor, Aimee was not willing to go to those extremes. She decided to push the furniture back from the center of the room and use tape and sea salt to create a pentagram. For one thing, it would protect her new floors, but additionally, the sea salt also served as an element from the earth and was considered a powerful conductor in spells.

"Seriously?" she asked. "You're actually going to sit on the ottoman while I push it across the floor?"

"If this spell works, I'm going to get you for this," she said with a smile as she pushed the ottoman away with all her might. It glided across the bare floor and slammed into the living room wall. Unfortunately, Martin was not affected by the action and continued to sit there, laughing.

Aimee realized that Martin's sense of fun and his light-hearted nature were two of the reasons she wanted to bring him back. Despite how hard his life was in the 1800's and what he endured in death, he never lost the true essence of who he really was. That was the man she wanted to spend the next three months with.

"I'm going to use tape and mark out the pentagram based on the dimensions I created. I cannot draw a straight line with a ruler, and to free hand this would be a disaster. I'm pretty sure the pentagram has to be exact and not a representation in order to make the spell effective," she said.

"Then what?" Martin asked.

"Then I will pour the 50 boxes of sea salt along the tape and create a perfect pentagram."

"You secured 50 boxes of sea salt!"

"Don't laugh. We will need all of it."

"Didn't anyone find it strange, you buying so much?"

"I'm sure they would have, but I didn't want to take the chance of someone asking me what it was for and then having to come up with a stupid answer, so I went to six different stores," she replied with a smile.

"Aimee, why did you put that point of the pentagram so close to the hearth?" Martin asked.

"According to Eliza, one of the points must represent fire. So I plan to light a fire in the fireplace instead of using a small candle. I want to make sure the Universe does not mistake my intentions."

"So, how will you represent the other elements?" he asked.

"Well, I will fill a crystal bowl with a shovel full of dirt from the garden to cover earth; I have another crystal bowl that will be filled with purified water; and wind will be represented by a battery-operated fan placed inside another crystal bowl. It will cause a slight breeze and thus represent wind."

"But, that only covers four of the pentagram points; what about the fifth?" he asked.

"Eliza said to place a bowl of crystals there as protection. I bought five crystal bowls and then ordered a variety of natural and polished crystals to place inside the final bowl. I'm pretty sure I've covered all five points to the best of my ability."

****

"The pentagram is done, what now?" Martin asked.

"You can keep me company in the kitchen while I crush the herbs to create the amulet bag I'm supposed to wear."

"I feel bad that I cannot help you do the work," Martin said.

"Don't worry about it, just having you keep me company is enough," she replied.

Aimee was glad that she had not taken the mortars and pestles to the antique store like she had initially planned when she found them in the Secret Pantry. Using the same tools the sisters used, ones that perhaps still held some of their powers, might help reinforce the strength of the amulet bag.

The first layer in the amulet bag was one of protection and activation of one's spirit guide. Aimee crushed the Rowan berries and placed them in the bag. She had also purchased two small wooden crosses made from the wood of the Rowan tree and placed one on top of the crushed berries. The next two layers were Yarrow and Thyme, for courage and love. Then she placed a layer of Rosemary for love and repelling negative energy. On top of that, she placed a layer of Lavender for protection, love and happiness. Aimee then repeated all the layers backwards, ending with the Rowan cross and crushed berries.

"I think you missed one of the herbs," Martin said, pointing to the bundle of dried sage still sitting on the counter.

"No, that is for cleansing the living room before we perform the ceremony. I'm supposed to light it, let it smolder and then say the cleansing spell Eliza left. She said it will also help protect us."

Aimee gathered the sage, amulet bag, Mary's dagger, and the locket and took them into the living room, where she would use them in a few hours.

"Martin, I'm going upstairs to watch a movie and try to rest. I really don't want to be stressed tonight and forget something and screw this whole thing up. I left your spell on the counter if you want to go over it a few more times. You are also welcome to join me for the movie."

"I'll join you," Martin said. "I've got my part memorized; it's you I'm concerned for."

"What? You think I'll screw it up?"

"No, that is not what I meant. I am concerned for you because this is asking a lot from you, and you are taking on a responsibility that you do not have to take on. I care about you and cannot bear to see you carry this much pressure alone."

"I'm not alone Martin. You are with me," she said.

"Do you recall the trip I took to Seattle for business? You were here by yourself for a week and I left the televisions on so you would not be lonely."

"Yes," he replied.

"Well I was the one that was lonely. I thought about you all day and wanted to call you in the evenings to talk; but knew you couldn't answer the phone. I worried that you would need help and no one would be there to help you. It was then I knew I was in love with you and all I wanted was your happiness. That is why I'm doing this Martin. It is not a burden because I love you."

****

Aimee didn't think she would fall asleep but when the alarm went off at 9PM, she was glad she had taken the initiative to set the alarm, otherwise she would have slept right past midnight and missed their opportunity.

"Do you feel better?" Martin asked.

"A little, I guess I was more tired than I realized."

Sitting up on the edge of the bed, Aimee asked, "So, what does one wear to a…a…what do we call what we are doing, Martin?"

"How about a birthday?" he replied.

"Very well, what does one wear to a re-birthday?" she asked, looking at Martin.

"Well, I'm stuck in this, but you could wear that pretty green dress you wore for the party you had for the New Year. You looked radiant in that dress," he said.

"The green dress it is. I'm going to get ready and I'll be down when I'm done."

Martin knew this was his cue to not only vanish, but to leave the room. "I'll be waiting," he said.

Aimee could see Martin sitting on the sofa as she descended the stairs. He was staring towards the pentagram. Once her last foot was on the foyer floor; the butterflies in her stomach began to fly around at record-breaking speeds. She went in and sat next to Martin.

"I was staring at the pentagram and I actually remember bits and pieces of that night. The sisters dragged me in here on a blanket. They were definitely too small to have carried me."

"That would explain why they painted the design. If they had used salt, then the design would have been destroyed when they dragged the blanket through it," Aimee commented.

"The only other thing I remember is looking up and seeing all three of them kneeling next to me, I think they were holding hands and singing, or chanting; I don't know."

May 1870 ~ Port Townsend

The moment that they were preparing for all week, with the utmost diligence, was at hand. A solemn hush fell over the house as the final stages began.

Eliza and Jane each held one corner of their parents' cherished Wedding Ring quilt and pulled Martin from the guest room at the back of the house to the front parlor. Once they had him positioned in the center of the pentagram and knew that they would not be disturbing him further, Eliza gave him a spoonful of Laudanum to dull the pain which they had created while moving him from room to room. His breathing was very shallow, and Eliza asked Jane to fetch a hand mirror so she could place it under his nostrils to check for signs that he was still alive. Time was running out.

While Eliza and Jane pinned copies of the crucial message Martin must remember on each wall in the house, Clair busied herself with bringing in the white candles that they had purchased for the ceremony. She placed them in a full circle around the outside of the pentagram and retreated to the kitchen to collect the herbs and bowls that she eventually placed on each of the five points of the pentagram. Before leaving the parlor, she lit the fire in the hearth to keep Martin warm.

Once everything was in place, the sisters returned to the kitchen and enjoyed their last few hours together. They reminisced about their childhood in Scotland, their mother, and the wonderful years they had spent in Port Townsend with their father. There were no regrets about what they had to do; in fact, it was the opposite. Eliza, Jane and Clair were relieved that they had finally been given the opportunity to fulfill their true purpose in life: to provide a second chance to someone deserving and to prevent the evil their mother unleashed, from becoming a permanent resident in this world.

Each sister studied the dark art spell one last time and then Eliza took the lid handle from the right side of the kitchen stove and placed it in the latch, she lifted the round cast-iron lid, exposing the fire inside. Sliding the papers into the fire, she returned the lid to the stove. The spell was extremely powerful, even for the most advanced witch, but to leave it unattended and allow it to fall into the hands of someone foolish enough to attempt it would be adding more punishment to their family.

When the grandfather clock struck half-past 11, the sisters picked up their personal daggers and they headed to the front parlor. Standing close, they held hands and formed a small circle. Bowing their heads, they shared a moment of silence as they each mentally said their final words. Hugging and kissing each other, the sisters stepped over the candles and into the inner circle where Martin and the pentagram lay.

Leaning over the candles, Jane grabbed a long, narrow piece of kindling and lit it in the hearth fire. She lit the candles that were nearest to her, and then she passed the flame to Clair and finally Eliza, who completed the circle and blew out the kindling. Taking their respective places on the pentagram, they kneeled. Eliza, as the eldest and strongest witch, kneeled on the top point, Jane to her left and Clair to her right.

Eliza lit the white sage and drew an imaginary circle of white light over the four of them, asking for guidance and protection from their spirit guides, and assistance from their mother and the members of her coven. She then tossed the sage into the hearth and anointed Martin's head with prepared oil from the small dish Clair had placed there earlier. The sisters held hands and waited for the first stroke of midnight.

On the final stroke of midnight, Clair released the hold she had on her sisters' hands and dipped her dagger in the bowl of herbs and oil they had prepared. With the dagger in both hands, she held it over Martin's body and began to chant the spell. On the final word of the incantation, Clair turned the dagger inward to her body, closed her eyes and ran the blade through her heart.

As Clair's body slumped forward, Eliza reached over and grabbed her youngest sister's hand and held it tightly as Jane began to perform the exact same ritual. Eliza then dipped her dagger and began the final step of the ceremony. Martin's body convulsed once, as if gasping for his last breath, and she knew she had to complete her spell before he died or Clair and Jane would have died for nothing. With swift and determined movement, Eliza pierced her heart and sealed the ritual.

The sky let out a pounding roar, then lit up with nonstop lightening. As the wind grew in intensity, the flames in the hearth shot upward through the chimney and were met by the violent wind, which pushed the flames back into the hearth, silencing them and distinguishing all light in the front parlor.

****

Ever since the night of the full moon, the skies had poured down on Port Townsend without a break. Everyone was forced to stay inside due to the powerful winds and mud created by the storm. Another week passed before anyone dared leave the protection of their homes.

Thomas Dew was the individual who volunteered to ride out to the Stuart Mansion to check on the sisters and take them fresh provisions, as the Stuart family was highly respected in their small community. This was a decision he regretted for the remainder of his life.

After repeated knocks on the front door, Mr. Dew decided to enter the house to make sure everything was okay.

"Hello. Miss Eliza, is anyone here? It's me, Mr. Dew from the general store. I thought I'd come out and see how you survived the big storm we've been having."

As he stepped further into the foyer, he was not greeted by what he expected, the usual "Good morning, would you like a cup of tea?" but by the sight of blood and bodies lying on the front parlor floor. Immediately turning around, Mr. Dew fled the Stuart Mansion and raced his horse back into town.

A telegram was immediately sent to the Constable in Seattle and the few details provided by Mr. Dew were relayed. Constable

Ragsdale informed the townspeople he would not be able to get any detectives across on the ferry for a few days because of the heavy wind and rain, but he doubted it would make any difference to the Stuart sisters.

****

The authorities from Seattle, a photographer, several volunteers from town and the undertaker left Port Townsend early on a May morning. The ground was now firm enough to hold the weight of the wagons without them getting bogged down in deep mud.

Everyone was prepared to find a murder scene, but what they weren't prepared for is what they did find: a sacrificial murder and triple homicide. Based on the rigidity of the corpses, the undertaker believed they had been there several weeks. The cold spring temperatures had kept the house cool enough to slow decay and allow for positive identification of the three women. However, the man was not from Port Townsend and no one had ever seen him before.

Photographs were taken of the crime scene and anything else Constable Ragsdale thought might shed some light on the situation. A photo was taken of the scene itself, one of the furniture piled in the dining room, one of the hand-written message that was pinned to every single wall in the house, and one of each bedroom, showing that the sisters had laid out their burial clothes on their respective beds and placed a suit on the bed in the guest bedroom for the gentleman on the floor.

No one knew what to make of this incident. The Stuart sisters had always been well liked in the small community and provided help to others when they could. The thought that they were luring men to their home and performing satanic rituals had shaken Port Townsend to its very core.

The local Pastor refused to allow their burial in the community cemetery, which was on consecrated land, and he refused to say a service over them. On the day of their burial, in the Stuart family cemetery, the only people present were the undertaker and the grave diggers. Once the task was completed, no one stayed to say any words over the sisters; they just wanted to get away from the evil place as fast as possible.

After reading the reply to his earlier telegram to Scotland in reference to the Stuart family, Constable Ragsdale sat motionless in his chair. The words 'demonic', 'evil' and 'witches' ran through his mind. The case was closed quickly as a sacrifice and triple suicide and never dealt with again. The disposal of the house and property was turned over to the Stuarts' solicitor who set the house on its long journey through time as a dark and misunderstood home.

Present Day ~ Port Townsend

"Well, hopefully Martin, in the morning you can sit here and look at that spot on the floor and have much different, happier memories," Aimee said as she looked into Martin's eyes.

Standing, Aimee said, "I'm sorry I cannot offer you one, but I need a very large glass of wine before we begin your re-birthday ceremony. I'll be right back."

When Aimee returned to the sofa, she was not only carrying a full glass of wine but the bottle as well.

"I wonder just how much Eliza and her sisters had to drink before they completed their ceremony. I'm not killing you, or myself, but I'm still freaked out. I have no idea what will happen and that scares the shit out of me," she said.

"I'm nervous too. I wonder if it will hurt," he began.

"Oh god, I didn't even think of that! Thanks, now I have something else to worry about!" she replied.

"I'm sorry, Aimee, I didn't mean to add to your burden. I don't care if it hurts as long as I come through from this world to your world and I can spend three months holding you."

Filling her wine glass one more time and quickly emptying the glass, Aimee set it on the table and stood. Shaking her arms as they hung at her side and rolling her shoulders, like a fighter preparing for his first round, she said, "Okay, we better get started. We are supposed to be in the center of the Pentagram on the first stroke of midnight."

Aimee first lit the fire, then poured the water and soil into their respective bowls and finished by turning on the portable fan and placing it in its bowl. She then lit the sage and motioned for Martin to stand next to her in the center of the pentagram. With the smoldering sage, she drew an imaginary circle of blessed white light around them and asked that they be protected as long as they were within the safety of the circle. Aimee then tossed the sage into the flames of the fire.

Bending over, she picked up the amulet bag and hung it around her neck. She then picked up the dagger and the locket. Opening the locket and cradling it in her left had to ensure the four locks of hair would not fall out, she steadied the dagger in her right hand.

"Alright, Martin, on the first stroke of 12, I will cut my hand with the dagger and let the blood fall into the locket. I will close the locket and put it around my neck, and then I will set the dagger down. After that, we will face each other and hold hands, or whatever it is we are capable of doing. After the final gong you begin chanting your spell and I will begin chanting my spell. Eliza did not leave any instructions after that step because I doubt they'd ever done this."

"Aimee," Martin said, "no matter what happens I want you to know I love you and will be eternally grateful for this moment."

"I love you too, Martin," she said as the grandfather clock in the foyer sounded the first of twelve gongs.

Aimee knew the instant the dagger sliced through her left palm that she was grateful she had consumed so much of the wine. Her eyes quickly shot up to Martin where he could see her pain. Holding the dagger and locket with her right hand, she allowed several drops of blood to soak the hair and then she closed the locket and put it around her neck as she bent over to set the bloody dagger on the floor.

Now facing Martin, Aimee realized she did not know how many gongs had passed. She had been so focused on what she was doing that she failed to count them. Looking up at Martin's face, she saw that he was mouthing nine, then ten; and she smiled. He had kept count.

On the eleventh gong, Martin reached over and took her hands. Although he could still pass through her, he held his hands still so they were barely inside Aimee's. She could feel the tingling of his spirit.

The final gong sounded and they began to repeat their respective spells. As Aimee focused on the words, she steadied herself by looking into Martin's eyes. He calmed her, gave her strength and a reason to continue. For a brief moment the tingling in her hands stopped and she felt the weight of another person touching her.

She became very light-headed but continued her portion of the spell, keeping her eyes locked on Martin. The fire exploded and then immediately died out, turning the room pitch black. Aimee could no longer feel Martin's hands or the tingling, and then an unknown force pushed through her body and she collapsed to the floor.

When she woke she realized she was lying across the pentagram, its design no longer recognizable. Getting to her feet, she went into the foyer and turned on the overhead light. The clock struck two o'clock.

"Oh my god, I was out for two hours!" she said with panic in her voice. Running from room to room, switching on the lights she called for Martin, expecting to find him lying somewhere in the house, but in the end she found nothing.

Returning to the foyer, she began to panic. What if Martin was unconscious and outside in the storm? Opening the front door, she pulled the amulet bag and locket from her neck and raced outside, into the violent storm, calling his name, searching in the cold night for her soul mate and fearing that they would never be together in this lifetime. In despair, Aimee knelt at the fence which separated her property from the public road. She held on with all her might and wept. Her despair was so deep that she did not feel the heavens crying down on her, draining the last bit of heat from her body.

"Aimee," she thought she heard the wind call, "Aimee." But it wasn't the wind, it was Martin.

"Martin!" she screamed out. "I couldn't find you and I thought you'd vanished forever."

When Martin reached Aimee he could see her body shaking from the cold. "We've got to get you inside and warmed up or you will catch your death from the cold. Then what will we do?" he stated as he reached down and picked her up from the ground.

At first Aimee's mind did not register what had just happened. Martin was no longer a ghost but a physical man and he was carrying her back into Stuart Mansion.

Carrying Aimee upstairs to her bathroom, he stepped into the shower and held Aimee as the warm water rained down on them. Holding her close, he hoped the warm water and his own body heat would bring the color back into her skin.

"I thought I'd lost you," Aimee said, looking up into Martin's eyes, her teeth chattering from the cold. "My heart broke and nothing seemed to matter."

He set Aimee down on her feet. "No, my love, you will never ever lose me," he replied, taking her face between his hands and kissing her.

Aimee felt the same tingling she felt when Martin's ghost tried to hold her hands, but this time she knew it wasn't caused by a ghost. It was the power of true love running through her body and awakening her soul.

Turning off the water, Martin said, "We need to get out of these wet clothes and under some warm blankets. I'm afraid you will catch your death from being out in the cold." Peeling off her wet clothes, Martin dropped them on the bathroom floor. Picking Aimee up in his arms, he carried her to the bed.

It didn't take long for the intense cold to leave Aimee's body as they huddled under the warmth of the blankets, their bodies intertwined.

As they kissed, Aimee realized she had never felt so at peace in her entire life. She felt complete, that a part of her had always been missing and now, with Martin lying next to her, she was whole. Carefully, Martin positioned himself above her body, trying not to crush her with his weight and he made love to her.

Martin laid there and watched Aimee as she slept; she looked so peaceful that he did not want to disturb her. She had gone through a lot last night. After a few minutes she opened her eyes and smiled.

"It wasn't a dream; you are really here!" she said as she caressed his cheek with her hand.

Leaning over and kissing her deeply, Martin asked, "Could a ghost do that?"

"No," she said, pulling him closer and whispering in his ear, "Just to make sure you are real, maybe you should show me a few more things that you could not do if you were still a ghost."

****

Martin had watched Aimee prepare her morning coffee for months now and figured he would surprise her by making coffee and bringing it to her in bed. When he returned to the bedroom, he found Aimee sitting up in bed.

"This time I didn't panic when I woke and found you gone. I could smell the coffee brewing and knew you were the one making it, since I forgot to prep it last night and set the timer," she said with a smile.

Walking over to her, Martin placed the steaming cup of coffee in her hands and kissed her on the top of her head.

"Do you have coffee too?" she asked, referring to the other cup in his hand.

"It smelled so good that I decided to try it. I prepared it just like yours and this is now my second cup," he said with a laugh, sitting on the edge of the bed next to her.

"See, I told you, the world cannot function without its morning coffee," she said, taking several sips and setting the cup on the night stand.

"So far everything Eliza told us would transpire once we performed the spell has happened," Aimee said.

"Yes, but it did take longer to reappear as a human than I thought it would," Martin replied.

"For a while there I thought we had failed and you had vanished forever. Now I'm nervous about what's going to happen at the end of the third full moon," she said.

"I do not believe they knew if it would actually work. It wasn't something they could practice, since they had to die to complete the initial spell," Martin replied. "From here on out, we are on our own."

"But you are here now! So, Martin Stuart, what would you like to do on your first day in this new world?" Aimee asked.

"I want to travel beyond the Stuart property. I want to ride in your vehicle and see what is out there."

"That's easy enough to accomplish. We can go for a drive and then have dinner somewhere interesting," she replied.

With her foot she nudged Martin. "Up," she said.

As Aimee flipped the covers back she stopped and looked at Martin. "I just had a terrible thought. What if you cannot go past the property line? I have no idea what the power or range of the spell is."

"Well, we will find out. If you travel over the property line and discover I'm no longer sitting next to you, then we know and we will come up with a new list of activities. Otherwise, we are going to see the world!" he replied with the enthusiasm of a small child.

"You do know you are walking around naked?" she said, stepping in very close to him and kissing him gently on the lips. "You are human now, and clothes left on, stay on, but no clothes on means you are naked," she said as she ran her hand down the length of his torso.

"My apologies, I did not realize…," he began.

"No need to apologize to me," she said with a big smile on her face, "but I thought I'd remind you so you don't find yourself wandering around town naked."

Aimee pulled the top blanket off the bed and wrapped it around her body. Picking up her cup of coffee, she walked into her closet and returned with a plastic bag.

"I thought you might need something to wear if the spell did work so I bought a pair of sweat pants, a t-shirt, socks, briefs and a pair of shoes. They are probably too big, but I was really guessing on your size. If we do make it past the property line, we will make the mall one of our stops today and get you some clothes that really fit you," Aimee said as she set the bag next to Martin on the bed.

"Aimee, do you mind if I use the washroom across the hall to get cleaned up while you are getting ready in here? I don't want to waste a minute of this day."

"No problem. I'll show you how to use the shower and where the extra towels are," Aimee said as she picked up the bag and headed towards her bedroom door and then to the guest bathroom across the hall.

****

"This is really strange for me; I can only imagine how you must be feeling," Aimee said as she pulled the car door shut and fastened her seat belt.

"My head is swimming," he replied as he mimicked Aimee's action with the door and seat belt.

Aimee started the engine and slowly drove the car from the circular drive to the dirt road that led to the paved County road which was the edge of her property. The dirt road was fairly smooth but periodically she would hit a hole and bounce Martin in his seat.

"So far so good," she commented, looking at Martin as she slowed the car and stopped just at the edge of the property line.

"Alright, Martin, you tell me when you are ready and I'll drive across the line."

"Now is good. I have no idea what will happen, but if I sit here much longer I will talk myself out of risking whatever might happen," he replied.

"Okay, on the count of three," she said as she placed the car back into drive and held her foot on the brake.

"One, two…," she counted and, without making it to three, stepped on the gas pedal, sending the car, without warning, across the invisible line, "…three!!" she concluded as she brought the car to a sudden stop.

Quickly looking to her right to see if Martin was still with her, she found him motionless. One hand was pressed against the dash board and the other gripped the door's arm rest. Placing her hand on his shoulder, Aimee gently shook him, "Martin, Martin, are you okay?" she asked.

Martin slowly turned his head towards her. "Aren't you supposed to say 'three' and then go?" he asked.

"Oh, that," she said, laughingly. "I didn't want you to panic and yell 'stop' when I got to three, so I just went for it. But look, you're still here. The spell gives you complete freedom!"

"Do you mind if I get out of the vehicle for a moment?" he asked.

"Sure, are you okay?"

"I just want to stand. I didn't realize how fast this thing went."

"Um, Martin, that was not fast, just sudden. I'll start slow to get you used to it, but in order for us to drive anywhere we have to go fast. Well, as fast as the law permits. Cars are very safe," she continued on, trying to ease the panic she could see on Martin's face. "Everyone has to take classes and pass tests before they are allowed to drive one."

Giving Martin a hug, she said, "Come on, get back inside; you will be fine."

"We're going 15 miles per hour, how you doing?" she asked. "Fine."

"Now we are at 30 miles per hour, you still doing okay?" she asked as she glanced at him.

Martin was sitting with his back pressed into the seat. His left hand was gripping the side of his seat and the right hand clenched the door rest.

"Here, let me unroll your window. Sometimes fresh air blowing on your face keeps you from feeling sick."

Aimee could tell Martin was stressed because he never questioned how his window just went down. "Breathe deep. You can close your eyes and try to relax or keep them open and look forward; otherwise you might get car sick."

Initially, Martin kept his eyes closed as Aimee slowly increased the speed from 30 up to 45 mph. By the time she reached 55, he had relaxed enough to let go of the side of his seat and open his eyes. Yet he continued to press his body into the back of the seat as if distancing himself from what was coming towards him on the road.

"How about we go to the mall first and you can get some new clothes. Plus, it will give you a break from the car?" she asked.

"That would be good. Maybe we can work up to a long drive later," he replied.

Once Martin was out of the car at the mall, his body became more relaxed. He stood next to the car for some time just looking at all the buildings and the sea of cars, both those that were parked in the parking lot, and those that continued traveling by on the roads. He was amazed at the synchronization of the traffic lights and perplexed at the lack of open land.

"Is everything like this? Busy, and full of buildings and people without any family homes and farms?"

"Pretty much. Small towns like this and large metropolitan cities are nothing but buildings, cars and people. Some people live in the cities, but most live in the suburbs or outside the city. There are huge areas of nothing but homes and parks for the kids to play in. Then there are large stretches of farms. Everything is really spread out because we have cars, trains, boats and planes to move around in."

Taking Martin's right hand in her left, she pulled him close to her side and then placed her right hand on his arm, to help him feel more secure. "Let's go inside the mall," she said as they started walking.

"If this becomes too much for you, just tell me. It will be busy with a lot of people and some will just be rude to you; don't take it personally. There's generally music playing in the main area of the mall and then each store will be playing their own music; trust me, it can be a little much at times. We can leave whenever you want."

"I'll be fine," Martin said. "I can't imagine it worse than fighting in the War."

"Then here we go," she said, opening the main door to the mall.

Aimee and Martin walked the full length of the mall to acclimate him to this new society. Martin's wide-eyed expressions and constant turning of his head to take everything in were like those of a child seeing something remarkable for the first time. She gave brief descriptions of what was sold inside each store and chatted about what people were wearing - or not wearing, and hair styles for men. When they reached the opposite end from where they started. Aimee suggested they go into The Gallery and check out the men's clothing.

Within two hours, the pair was headed back to Aimee's car to drop off Martin's new wardrobe. Aimee wished it was that easy for a woman to buy an entire wardrobe: one stop, one shop and done! After they secured the packages, Martin wanted to return to the mall and have Barber Buzz cut his hair.

"Martin, are you sure you want to do this?" Aimee asked as they re-entered the mall and walked to the barber shop.

"Yes, I want to look modern like everyone else," he said as they signed in at the shop's front desk.

"But you don't want to do something you will hate and be stuck with for eternity," she said as the barber approached them.

"I take it his hair grows really slowly," the barber said. "It looks like it hasn't been cut in ages."

Both Martin and Aimee laughed.

"Sorry, inside joke," Aimee said, looking over to Martin.

"Martin, you've had long hair forever; it's all you've known and I would feel terrible if you were stuck with something you hated."

"He's in good hands, Miss. You will both like the look when I'm done," the barber said as he led Martin away.

When Martin emerged from the barber shop, Aimee did not recognize him at first. His hair was cut just above his shoulders and it was all one length. It framed his strong jawline perfectly, and she never realized how blue his eyes were when his hair had been pulled back tight against his scalp. Setting her magazine down on the table, Aimee walked over to him and ran her fingers through his hair.

"Now, this is a very modern and sexy look for you," she said and winked.

"I'm glad you approve, since you are the one I am trying to impress," he said with a smile.

Placing his hand on Aimee's arm, Martin asked, "Do you mind if we go home now?"

"Is everything okay?" she asked.

"Honestly, I feel very strange. I cannot explain it, but I think we should go home."

This time Aimee did not ease Martin into the experience of riding in a car. She put the car in reverse and headed to the nearest exit. She changed lanes often to pass slower moving vehicles and ran every yellow light she hit. Once she was on the highway, she didn't care what the speed limit dictated, she was going as fast as she could to get Martin home.

When she looked over at him, thinking he would have a look of terror on his face, she discovered he was sleeping. Aimee couldn't decide if that was a good sign or a bad one.

Pulling into the circular drive and parking the car, she reached over to wake Martin.

"Sweetie, we're home," she said, but he did not move. Getting out of the car and running around to his door, she opened it and removed his seat belt.

Placing her hands on his shoulders, she shook him. "Martin! Wake up, Martin!" Slowly he opened his eyes.

Aimee began to panic. He was not acting normal, but more like someone coming out of anesthesia; groggy and disoriented. She also noticed the color was draining from his skin.

"Come on honey, you've got to help me a little here. We need to get you inside and upstairs to bed," she said as she grabbed his legs and swung them out of the car. "You need to stand and try to walk."

The ascent up the front stairs to the main door was daunting. Although Martin's legs worked, he stumbled with each step and Aimee was forced to stabilize his dead weight against her small body. She dreaded the climb up the grand staircase, but needed to get him into bed where he could be comfortable.

Each step gripped her heart with fear. Something had gone wrong with the spell and he was dying again. By the time she had him safely in bed she was crying so hard she could barely breathe.

Kissing his forehead she said, "I'll be right back. I need to get Eliza's stuff and figure out what I missed."

Martin grabbed her hand, "I love you, Aimee," he said.

"I love you too, Martin," she said as she leaned over and kissed him. Wiping her tears from his face, she ran out of the room and upstairs to the nursery to retrieve Eliza's letters and her book of spells.

When Aimee returned to the bedroom, Martin was asleep. She sat on the bed next to him so she could monitor his breathing, which was very faint and shallow. Opening the book to the page marked by the white ribbon, Aimee picked up the letter and instructions that Eliza had left for her. Carefully rereading their contents, she hoped to find some clue as to what went wrong. God willing, Aimee hoped to find a way to fix the problem.

As she read the instructions and spell, she mentally retraced her steps from the night prior. She did follow Eliza's instructions exactly, prior to the ritual, except she did not burn the dark arts spell. Running downstairs to the kitchen, she grabbed the papers and a box of matches and ran into the living room where she lit the papers on fire and burned them in the fireplace. Once they were nothing but ash, she ran back upstairs and sat with Martin, looking and waiting for any change in his condition.

Not knowing how much time he had left, she decided she could not wait any longer. Brushing his hair back from his face, she kissed him and said, "I'm going downstairs for a minute. I want to walk through everything I did last night. I missed something and I need to figure it out. I'll be right back."

Martin did not stir.

Standing in the center of what was left of the salt pentagram, Aimee began her mental walk-through of the previous night's ritual. She lit the sage, drew the circle and tossed the sage in the fire. So far, so good, she thought. Then she leaned over and picked up the dagger, which she used to cut her palm and drip blood into the locket. The dagger was still on the floor.

"The locket!" she said out loud and automatically reached for the chain that should have been around her neck. "Where is the locket?!"

Dropping to her knees, she began to scan the floor around the salt design. She ran her hands through the disturbed piles of salt and looked in the crystal bowls, but found nothing. Crawling across the floor, she looked under all the furniture in the living room but did not find the locket.

Running back up to her bathroom, she found the still-wet clothes she was wearing the night prior piled on the floor, and next to them was Martin's burial suit. Shaking the articles of clothing and finding nothing, she began looking under the bedroom furniture. When the locket was still not discovered she shook Martin awake.

"Martin, it's the locket. When you brought me upstairs and took off my clothes, what did you do with the locket?" she asked.

Martin shook his head slowly from side to side and said in a very faint voice, "You weren't wearing the locket or the bag."

"I've got to find the locket before it's too late," she said as she rushed out of the room and back to the living room. Taking a deep breath, she tried to recall what happened after she woke, and discovered that she was lying on the floor. All she could remember was the panic of not finding Martin and running through the house looking for him, but then running outside and ending up at the wrought-iron fence, where Martin found her.

Aimee searched every inch of the front porch and the path she believed she took to the fence, but still she could not find the locket. Bursting into tears, she ran back into the house. Shutting the front door, she leaned against it and slid down to the floor, where she sat and cried.

Angry with herself for not finding the locket, she began pounding the back of her head against the front door. When the pain became too much, she simply slumped down on the floor and curled up into a ball. That is when she saw it.

Wedged between the front entry table and the wall, lost in the shadows of the foyer, was the locket. Crawling over to the table, she pulled it away from the wall and retrieved the locket. Placing it around her neck, she then raced up the stairs and curled up next to Martin.

If it was too late, she wanted to spend his last moments holding him. The hours dragged by and Martin slowly regained his strength. Aimee had fallen asleep and did not realize he was healed until he kissed her passionately, waking her up.

"It worked!" she said, wrapping her arms around his neck. "I will never take this locket off again!"

"I hate it when someone gives you their secret cookie recipe and leaves out a crucial ingredient or step, just so you cannot duplicate their cookies, and they remain the only one who can make them correctly," she said, laughing.

"I'm sure Eliza did not leave out the fact that you have to keep the locket with you at all times on purpose," Martin replied.

"No, I don't think so either. She and her sisters had a lot on their minds. I'm just grateful I was able to figure it out in time and save you."

"I'm the one who is grateful," Martin said as he ran his hand down her torso and to the inside of her thigh. "If you don't have any other adventures planned for today, I'd like to show you just how grateful."

****

Every morning Martin performed the same routine: he would go into the garden and cut a single bloom and bring it back inside and present it to Aimee. She placed the first one in a vase on the table by her bedroom window. As the days passed she had to find a larger vase and the single bloom grew into a beautiful bouquet.

"You know what I want to do today?" Aimee asked, placing this morning's Lily in the vase.

"What would that be?" Martin replied.

"Let's start planting in the herb and flower beds," she replied. "You said you wanted to be a farmer when you got to Washington, well, here's your chance. You can do the hard work and I'll bring you iced tea," she said, laughingly.

"No seriously, we can do it together. It will be something for me to have of us, once you are a ghost again."

"I think it's a great idea. We can also get the vegetable garden going so you can have food this winter," he replied.

"We will need to go to Home-Savers and purchase garden tools. We should be able to get most of the starter plants there too," she said.

Aimee was excited to replicate Clair's gardens. She knew they were too extensive to complete in one season, but with Martin's help she would be able to get a significant portion planted. So far, the bulbs she planted last fall were all growing right on schedule. In a few years, she should have a sea of early spring flowers once the bulbs divided a few more times.

"Hand me the shovel and I'll do the digging," Martin said. "It's the least I can do after you wore yourself out breaking through the wall upstairs."

Planting and harvesting were Aimee's favorite parts of gardening. All the hard work that goes into it before you plant and at the end of the season were required, but she did not enjoy doing it. She was more than happy to let Martin take charge of the manual aspect of gardening.

Within a week the garden beds were planted, but Martin did not want to stop there. He wanted to plant white roses along the path that led from the house to the family cemetery and then plant a large circular flower bed in the front, with dark roses on the outside and two white rose bushes in the center, to represent their love.

Aimee suggested they select two of Clair's rose choices from her journal. They settled on the Madame Hardy, with its snow-white appearance and delicate design, for the path and center of the circle. The Tuscany Superb, with its deep crimson, velvety blooms, was selected for the outer circle of the bed in the front yard. Aimee found a seller online that could ship the live plants to them within 48 hours.

Martin wanted to leave Aimee with as many things as he could, to help her feel connected to him once he was gone. As much as he wanted to be part of her life forever, he knew it was wrong to trap her, a living, breathing soul, in a house with a ghost. He knew what needed to be done, but dreaded the moment he had to carry it out.

****

"What are you up to this morning?" Aimee asked Martin when she entered the kitchen.

"I'm just looking through Jane's recipes. My mother used to make a lot of these."

"Why don't you select a couple of them and then we can go to the grocery store in town and get whatever ingredients we need."

"I would like that," Martin replied. "I've been longing for some good old home cooking."

"Excuse me," Aimee said with a chuckle, "are you saying that my cooking is bad?"

"You know exactly what I mean," Martin said as he winked at her.

"Do you know how to cook?" Aimee asked.

"No, not at all. I can bring home the fish and meat, but I've never prepared it to eat. To be honest, if I had all the time in the world, I would really like to learn to cook. I love to watch you take all the ingredients and turn them into a fantastic meal. It's art."

"Well, thank you. I think we have enough time today to give you a few cooking lessons," she replied.

"You keep looking and let me know what you decide on when I come back downstairs," she said as she poured a cup of coffee and headed out of the kitchen.

Martin wished he had a hundred days so he could try every one of Jane's recipes. It was so hard to select a favorite among dishes like Guinea Fowl Pudding, Haggis, and Minced Beef Cobbler.

Martin's mouth began to water as he recalled the wonderful tastes of these dishes.

"So, what did you select for dinner today?" Aimee asked as she returned to the kitchen.

"It was not easy, but I would like to prepare Cock-a-Leekie Soup, Hogmanay Steak Pie and Cranachan for dessert."

"I've heard of the soup, but what is Hogmanay Steak Pie and Cranachan?"

"Hogmanay is the Scottish word used to refer to the last day of the year. So, it would be a New Year's Eve steak pie. The Cranachan is a sweet cream, oat and fresh berry dish. It also contains whiskey and is a traditional dish to finish off your Burns Supper."

"I'm sorry, what is a Burns Supper?" Aimee asked.

"My parents grew up in Scotland and brought many of the traditions with them to America. One of them was the Burns Supper, which is a celebration of the life of poet Robert Burns. The supper is held on January 25th, the eve of his birthday."

"That is very interesting," Aimee said, "and it makes the meal more authentic, knowing the history of the dishes. Hand me the recipe book and I'll write down what we need to buy."

After they stopped at the local farmer's market and then the grocery store for the final ingredients, Aimee headed to the liquor store so they could purchase an authentic Scottish Whiskey. Placing the whiskey on the counter, the clerk, Denise said, "Now that is a big change from your usual purchases, Aimee."

Looking down at the large bottle, sitting on the counter in front of her, Aimee laughed and replied, "It's still for a new recipe, but my boyfriend likes to drink whiskey, so the rest is for him."

Once they were outside, Martin said, "So, I'm your boyfriend," as he smiled at Aimee.

"Get over yourself," she said as she kissed him on his cheek.

"What did the girl mean when she said this purchase was a big change for you?" Martin asked.

"Everyone in that store knows I only by small sample bottles of liquor when I'm trying a new recipe. They joke that I buy my liquor by the Tablespoon. It's just that I don't want to waste money on something I don't normally drink, and if I don't like the finished dish, well then, the liquor would be wasted."

When they returned from town, Aimee instructed Martin and they worked together to prepare the special meal. Martin followed her instructions and genuinely seemed to enjoy the cooking process.

Aimee set a romantic table for them in the kitchen. She placed candles on the table and poured a different wine to accompany each course. She could tell Martin was very pleased with the outcome of the dishes.

"This is the one thing I will miss when I'm a ghost again."

"What is that?" Aimee asked.

"The wonderful smell and taste of food; it is a very comforting experience."

Standing up from her chair and walking over to where Martin was sitting, Aimee tapped her foot against the back leg of his chair, indicating she wanted him to scoot back from the table, and then she straddled him on the chair and faced him.

"Seriously, food is the one thing you will miss when you are a ghost?" she said as she ran her hands through his hair and gently kissed his face.

It only took a few moments of her grinding her pelvis on his groin for her to know what he was really going to miss. "No, my love, you will be the only thing I miss," Martin said as he kissed her long and hard while he pulled her body into his.

****

Aimee was nervous. This was the first, and most likely last time Sarah and Peter would get to meet Martin. It will be difficult enough, at the end of the three months, to be without Martin in his physical form, but then to add the burden of explaining to everyone why he is gone, it was just too much. Aimee loved Martin and really wanted her sister to know him as she does, but knew it meant creating a lie about him once he vanishes.

Martin could sense her apprehension. Taking her by the hand, he turned her around to face him so he could look into her eyes and reassure her.

"Are you afraid something will be said that leads to them finding out who I really am?" he asked.

"No, well, maybe a bit," she said. "I'm just tense because I know I will have to lie to my sister and then, when you are gone, I'll have to lie again."

"Why don't you go without me and spend the evening with your family?"

"No, Martin, we have so few days left as it is, and I want to spend every moment with you. Either way I will be telling her a lie, so I would prefer they at least get to meet you and see how wonderful you are."

With that said, Martin pulled Aimee tightly against his body and wrapped his arms around her. She could feel his heart beating in his chest, feel the warmth of his body against hers and she felt safe and loved in his arms. She wanted to hold on to this moment, to this feeling for the rest of her life, but she knew it would end and there was absolutely nothing she could do about it…nothing!

"I love you, Aimee, and nothing else matters," he said, holding her face between his hands and gently kissing her. "Please don't be sad; let's go and make some great memories that we can both hold on to in the end."

"I love you too Martin, and you're right; it is what it is, and we need to enjoy every single moment together."

The Sailor's Street Fair and Dance was an annual event in Port Townsend and Aimee had been looking forward to this year's event since she missed last year's. Aimee and Martin decided to walk from Stuart Mansion into town because it was a beautiful summer afternoon. Sarah and Peter were arriving on the 3PM ferry and they planned to visit the vendors' booths, have something to eat, and then enjoy a night of street dancing and listening to the live music.

They reached the dock just as Sarah and Peter were exiting the ferry. When Sarah caught sight of Aimee, she grabbed Peter's hand and dragged him along as she ran towards her sister. Stopping in front of Aimee, Sarah immediately let go of Peter and gave her sister a big hug.

"We've missed you," Sarah said. "It's been months since we last got together."

"Oh, I am sorry, Sis, just with work and trying to learn everything I can about the house and then planting the gardens, well, time just got away from me."

Still holding onto her sister, Sarah looked over to Martin and said, "Sweetie, it looks like you've been far busier than you've been letting on!"

Letting go of Sarah's hands, Aimee placed her arm around Martin's arm. "Martin, this is my sister Sarah and her husband Peter. Guys, this is Martin McDonald."

"It's nice to meet you," Sarah and Peter said in unison.

Aimee laughed, "See, that's what happens when you're married. You talk as one."

"Martin must be a popular name in Scotland," Peter commented.

"Why do you say that?" Martin asked.

"Well, I'm sure Aimee has shown you her beloved cemetery. One of its residents is also named Martin."

"Yes, she has," Martin said, "I think it's great that she cares so much for a group of people she has never met. I believe that

Martin is a Stuart and I'm a McDonald, but yes, the name Martin generally occurs once or twice in every family."

Aimee realized she was right to be nervous over the introduction of Martin to her family, because they loved him. Sarah found him charming and handsome while Peter seemed to have found a long-lost friend. Aimee's stomach began to turn; how would she get through this when Martin leaves?

Pushing the depressing thoughts from her mind, Aimee was determined to enjoy every moment with Martin. Grabbing Sarah's hand, she said, "Come on everyone, let's go find where those delicious smells are coming from. I'm starving."

"That's Aimee in a nutshell," Sarah said, laughingly.

"What do you mean?" Martin asked.

"This girl has a bottomless pit when it comes to any type of festival food. When we were kids and our parents would take us to the State Fair, Pat and Mom would go look at the animals and exhibits, while Dad and I stayed with Aimee as she ate her way down the food alley."

"Hey, no telling childhood secrets, or I might have to tell Peter something about you," Aimee laughed.

"I'm on Aimee's side here," Peter said. "You only live once so let's go see what we can eat."

Martin looked at Aimee and they started laughing at Peter's comment.

"Aimee, I'm so happy you finally found someone," Sarah said. "You two seem genuinely happy with each other."

"We are Sarah; it's wonderful," Aimee replied.

"Good thing I'm married or I'd be jealous. He is one fine looking man, and that ass of his…"

"Sarah!" Aimee said, "You've definitely had too much to drink. Don't make me tell your husband you're drooling over my boyfriend."

"Why don't you two come to Seattle next weekend? You can stay with us and we could go to a play or something," Sarah suggested.

"We'd love to Sarah, but Martin has to fly back to Scotland next weekend."

"What's he doing there?" Sarah asked.

"He has to close out his father's estate. He'll be gone a few weeks, but when he gets back, I'm sure we can definitely come and visit," Aimee replied.

****

The last few days of the third and final month were passing far too quickly. Each morning when Aimee woke, she felt a dread in the pit of her stomach because they were one day closer to the end.

"I have a surprise for you; Martin," she said, giving him a long hug and breathing in his essence.

"And what might that be? Did you find a way to extend my vacation?" he asked jokingly.

"I wish I could, but no," she said. "We're going to the Port Townsend Cemetery."

"Are you trying to get rid of me?" he asked.

"Oh, you are so funny," she said, playfully poking him in the stomach.

"Remember the night we first met, you told me about your friend Henry and that you never knew what happened to him?"

"Yes."

"Well, I hired a professional genealogist and gave him as much information as I had from you. I got a call last night that Henry Baker has been located. It seems he did eventually return to Port Townsend; you had been dead about two years. He met a girl and, a few years later left the Windspur, and settled down here in the community as a farmer. He's buried in the local cemetery."

Martin's eyes filled with tears. "You did that for me?" he asked.

"I wanted to help you fill in the missing pieces, and I know that discovering what happened to Henry was very important to you."

Pulling Aimee in close and kissing her, he said, "Do you have any idea how much I love you?"

"Hopefully as much as I love you," she replied with a smile.

"I thought we could stop at the flower shop and buy some flowers for his grave, if you would like."

"Yes, I want to pay my respects properly," Martin replied.

When they reached the historical cemetery, Aimee parked the car on the little dirt road just inside the gate. It was a small cemetery compared to the historical ones she'd seen in Boise, but it turned out to be larger than she thought once they started walking from headstone to headstone, looking for Henry's grave.

After an hour they finally found a small marker with the inscription 'Henry Baker 1895' and a small saying, 'I hope the farm met your expectations Martin' written on it. Martin knelt down and placed the flowers next to the decaying marker. He sat there quietly for a few minutes, then stood and wiped the tears from his eyes.

"Thank you, Aimee, you will never know how much this means to me," he said as he kissed her and took her hand in his. "Let's go home and spend the rest of our time together."

****

When they woke on the final morning, the sky was dark and it was raining.

"I guess I'll be going out the same way I came in…" Martin said, "in the rain."

"You do know the rule for a dark, rainy day, don't you?" Aimee asked.

Looking at her with a puzzled expression on his face, he said, "No."

"You light a fire and then we spend the entire day in bed, making love. You have to, it's a rule," she said.

Getting out of bed, Martin walked over to the fireplace, started a fire and then returned to bed.

"Well, if it's a rule, then we must follow it," he replied as he kissed her and pulled her body on top of his.

The time flew by too quickly and the grandfather clock in the foyer struck 10PM. "I guess I should get ready," Martin said.

"What do you mean?"

"Well, I don't think you want me to go through eternity naked. I thought we could take a shower together and then you could select the clothes you want to see me in day after day after day.

"Oh, that's an easy pick: the faded blue jeans, brown dress shoes, and the white dress shirt. You look so handsome in those clothes," she said.

"Well, you get the clothes ready and meet me in the shower," he replied.

Martin had his back to Aimee when she entered the shower. She stood right behind him and ran her nails gently up and down his back while kissing his body. He turned around and kissed her deep and long. As he lifted her up off the floor, she wrapped her legs around his waist and Martin backed her up to the shower wall. They made love like wild animals, desperate in their desire because they both knew it was the last time they would ever be together. It was hard to tell if the water running down their faces was strictly from the shower or a combination of water and their tears.

Once Martin was dressed, they both lay back down on the bed and held each other, waiting for the final stroke of midnight and whatever was going to happen.

Martin took Aimee's left hand and slid his mother's wedding ring on her finger and said, "If things were different I would marry you and spend the rest of our lives together. I love you more than words can say, Aimee Morgan."

Tears filled Aimee's eyes, "I love you too, Martin, and I would definitely accept your proposal."

Martin kissed her one last time. Neither spoke, they just held on to each other tightly, perhaps hoping that their hold on each other would prevent the Universe from snatching Martin back into his solitary existence. Exhaustion finally overtook both of them. When Aimee woke the following morning, Martin was gone.

****

"Aimee, Paul and I are really worried about you. You haven't returned my calls in over a week. Is everything okay?" Sarah asked.

Aimee could no longer hold out hope that Martin would reappear. It had been a week since the end of the third full moon and the morning flowers had stopped. She was happy in the thought that he was now at peace, and no longer subject to the imprisonment of the Stuart Mansion, but her heart was broken at the same time. She truly loved him and wanted to spend the rest of her life with him by her side, even if he was a ghost.

"Sarah, Martin is gone," Aimee replied.

"What do you mean, gone?"

"He was killed in a car crash while in Scotland. Sarah, he is never coming back."

"Oh, Honey, I am so sorry. I don't know what to say," Sarah replied. "Hold tight, I'm going to catch the next ferry over. I'll be there as soon as possible."

Maybe it was best to have Sarah stay with her for a while, at least she could talk to her about Martin and have time to grieve; otherwise, she would have to keep him a secret in her heart forever and that was just too much of a burden to ask anyone to carry.

"I made you a grilled cheese, just the way you like it," Sarah said, as she set the plate on the nightstand next to Aimee. "You really need to eat something, even a few bites."

"I know what I should do, and what other people have done to get through this, but I don't believe I have it in me, Sarah. He was my soul mate. You only find that person once in a lifetime, and we were together so briefly."

"Aimee, you will love again," Sarah replied.

"Yes, loving someone is easy, but finding the individual who connects with you on such a deep level that it can cross time, well that, that is only something that you can find with your soul mate."

Holding up her left hand, Aimee showed Sarah the ruby ring that had belonged to Martin's mother. "We were going to announce our engagement once he returned from Scotland. He gave it to me the night before he left," she said.

"Wow, it's beautiful. It looks really old," Sarah replied.

"It's been in his family since the 1820's; it belonged to his great-great grandmother, or something like that."

Aimee knew it was a lie, the bit about announcing their engagement. Martin did, however, promise to be with her forever and he gave her the ring as a symbol of his eternal love. Aimee needed her sister to see her loss as more than a three-month relationship that ended. She needed someone to understand the depth of her loss and sorrow.

Sarah stayed with her sister, cradling her when she cried, sharing her memories of Martin and helping her accept the pain so she could move forward. Aimee had always been the strongest of the three Morgan sisters. She would stand up for the less fortunate and hold her head high even when she felt like doing the opposite. Martin's death had affected her profoundly and Sarah was not sure if she would truly recover.

Time passed and Aimee did not improve. Her depression was compounded by the flu and severe dehydration, which forced Sarah to call for an ambulance to take Aimee to the hospital, where they fed her saline and nutritional fluids intravenously for several days.

"How are you feeling today, Miss Morgan?" the doctor asked as he glanced over her chart and replaced it on the hook at the end of her bed.

"Better, I guess," she replied.

"Well, your vitals are back to normal, but I am concerned about your depression and with the baby, I think it's best to have you speak with someone before we let you go home."

"Excuse me?" Aimee blurted out. "What baby?"

"Miss Morgan, you are 14 weeks along. Haven't you seen your doctor yet?" he asked.

"No, I didn't know I was pregnant!"

"Then it looks like we need to have you talk with a few more people before we let you leave here," he replied.

When Sarah and Peter arrived for their daily visit, they were shocked at the change they saw in Aimee. She was sitting up in bed, chatting away on the phone to their mother, and happier than they had seen her since the accident.

"Well, what brought on this remarkable transformation? Not that I am not thrilled, but yesterday when I left, you were in tears," Sarah asked as she leaned over to give her sister a hug.

"I'm pregnant! Can you believe it? I'm 14 weeks pregnant. I may have lost Martin, but he will live on in our child."

"Oh Aimee, that is wonderful news," both Sarah and Peter said in unison. It made everyone laugh at how connected they were in their thoughts.

"The doctor wants me to stay a couple more days so I can get set up with an OB doctor, and he wants me to speak with a counselor about my depression," Aimee stated.

"Sounds like a good idea, Aimee," Sarah said. "I'm thrilled for you and so glad to have you back to your beautiful, happy self."

The moment Aimee got home she ran through the house. "Martin, I'm pregnant, we are going to have a baby. I hope you can hear me; we are going to be parents."

Aimee did not care what her actions might look like to others, because she truly believed that somehow, somewhere, Martin would hear her and he would know that he was living on in their child.

The pregnancy gave Aimee time to rest. She hadn't really realized it, but she had been on the go since she returned from Sarah and Peter's at Thanksgiving with the first bits of information about her new home. She had spent the past five months working to give Martin three months of life and now, in a few months, she will be bringing their child into the world. Funny how the Universe works, Aimee thought.

With a baby on the way, Aimee thought it would be fun to use the third-floor children's nursery as a reading and games room for the new child. She wanted it restored exactly as it had been left by the Stuart family, partly because she wanted to preserve the memory of Martin's home, but also to provide him a safe place, should he ever return. Aimee had all the children's furniture including, chairs, easels, a table where they took their meals and afternoon tea, and the doll beds removed and taken to a local wood worker who would refinish each piece and return them to the nursery. The fireplace would be purely decorative this time around, and the secret room would remain as such, a secret.

Aimee decided to utilize the remainder of the space where the servants' quarters had once been as a theatre room and giant, indoor playground for the child to use, when the weather was too nasty to play outside.

Aimee loved the quality of work that Paul Fredrickson and his crew did on the main house, but she was unable to use them for the third-floor renovation due to other obligations. To her surprise, a local renovation company was eager to offer its services for the project, and it turned out to be a husband and wife team.

Aimee found it rather strange that the wife, Noni, spent more time sitting and thinking then actually working. Every time Aimee would check on the progress, she would find Noni sitting in a corner, apparently thinking, while her husband and the other two men they brought in were hard at work.

The work on the third floor progressed quickly and Aimee was eager to have the workers gone. The noise of their tools echoed through the house and she found it difficult to rest. It was near the end of the project when Aimee discovered what Noni's actual role was. Apparently, she was a psychic, or claimed to be one, and convinced her husband to let her tag along so she could get a reading on the Stuart Mansion.

Aimee was resting on the sofa in the living room when Noni entered the room. "Excuse me, Aimee, if I'm not interrupting, could I speak with you?" Noni asked.

"Sure, take a seat," Aimee said, sitting up and motioning for her to sit down beside her.

"I don't know if you are aware of this, but I am a psychic."

"Really," Aimee said matter of fact.

"I can see those who have passed on, those who are trapped between the afterlife and our world."

"Can you talk to them?" Aimee asked eagerly, but not with any real interest in Noni's answer.

"No, unfortunately I can only see them. I can also sense their feelings and emotions, but I have never actually been able to speak with them," she replied. "To be honest, I'm not sure if anyone can actually hold a conversation with a ghost, since they are made of energy and thought and they are not a physical being."

"Interesting," Aimee said, "but why are you telling me this?"

"I'm sure you are fully aware of the history of your house, but I thought you might want to know what I've learned since I've been here with my husband."

"Well, let's go into the kitchen and I'll make us some tea, and you can tell me what you have learned about my house and how you came to have such a unique name," Aimee said.

The two ladies sat at the breakfast table and Noni began to explain to Aimee that her parents were holistic healers and truly believed in the power of certain healing plants, one of them being the Noni, or Indian Mulberry, so they decided to name her after that particular plant.

"I think they were expecting me to become a healer like them, but I had other plans," Noni concluded.

"Well, picking a name for your child is not easy, that's for sure," Aimee replied.

"Have you selected any names for your baby?" Noni asked.

"If it's a boy, then I will name him after his father, Martin. If I have a girl, I plan to name her Lily, because that was the last flower her father brought me before he passed away."

"Those are both wonderful names, with powerful meanings," Noni replied.

"So tell me, Noni, what have you learned about this house," Aimee said.

Noni began to explain that the house was haunted by the spirits of the three Stuart sisters. She said they were trapped between realms because they were so evil that they could not cross over to heaven or hell. She also warned Aimee that she should have an exorcism performed on the house before the baby is born.

"I've been in this house for nearly a year, and nothing strange has ever happened. Why would the sisters stay silent for that length of time, but become active now that there is a baby on the way?" Aimee asked.

"They want the child. It's common knowledge in the paranormal circle that witches who perform sacrifices, like the Stuart sisters did, require newborn babies to strengthen their powers."

"Really!" Aimee said, trying to act surprised and concerned at the same time. "What on earth could they possibly be strengthening their powers for, after all this time?"

"It is very hard to say. Maybe they think they can take human form again," Noni replied.

Aimee did her best to keep a straight face. She took a sip of tea every time she wanted to smile at the comments. If the sisters really were hanging out, it would have been nice for them to intervene when Martin started dying because she didn't have the locket in her possession. How hard would it have been for one of them to appear and say, "Honey, you need to get the locket from the foyer and wear it around your neck, or the connection will be lost and he will die forever."

"Did you learn anything else?" Aimee asked.

"I know there is an angry spirit in this house, besides the sisters. I do not know who it is, but every time I come here I feel its anger. It feels like it does not want me here."

Aimee knew exactly how the 'spirit' felt, because she really did not want Noni there either. Noni was not a bad person, but Aimee felt violated having a so-called psychic prying around her house making up stories about what was going on. No doubt, this information would become common knowledge in town before the day was over.

"Oh my god," Noni gasped as she wrapped her arms around her chest, "did you feel that?"

No. I didn't feel anything," Aimee replied.

"An intense cold just went through my body, like someone swung a blade through me several times."

"Honestly, Noni, I did not feel anything. Perhaps you should go, especially if there really is a spirit who is angry with you. I would hate for anything to happen to you," Aimee replied as she extended her hand to hold Noni's.

"Yes. Yes, I think I will. No one else seems to be disturbed by this presence, just me."

While Aimee lay in bed that night, she felt at peace. Somehow, some way, Martin was still there watching out for her. The fact that none of the workers had been bothered, just the busy body-psychic, told her it was Martin getting rid of the people he didn't like in their home. With that knowledge, Aimee slept better that night than she had in months.

****

Aimee had planned to meet Sarah and Lily for lunch, once she finished at the doctor's office, and the three of them were going to the aquarium and for some quality, girls' time shopping. Unfortunately, Aimee did not feel like doing anything but going home and crawling into bed and crying. Her emotions were a mix of anger, fear and hatred for the Universe. What was she supposed to do with news like this, and what was going to happen to Lily?

When Aimee reached the bistro, Sarah and Lily were already seated and laughing about some silly thing. Aimee did not want to spoil that happiness so she took a deep breath, pulled her shoulders back and joined her family at the table.

"Mind if I join you?" Aimee asked with a bright smile, but Sarah knew her sister well enough to know something was just not right. She did not press Aimee for the information; she knew she would tell her when the time was right.

"Mommy, after I eat all my lunch, can we go over there and get ice cream?" Lily asked as she pointed to the little ice cream shop across the street from the bistro.

"I'm pretty sure we can squeeze that in," Aimee said as she leaned over and kissed her daughter on the head.

Despite the dark shadow looming over Aimee's spirit, she truly enjoyed the afternoon with her sister and daughter. Aimee loved to watch Lily when she experienced something new for the first time; it always reminded her of the joy Martin showed when he did the same. Aimee wished Martin could have been able to remain a ghost in the house, just to have the opportunity to watch their daughter grow. Just as she and Lily were about to board the ferry and return to Port Townsend, Aimee leaned in close to Sarah and said, "Sarah, please call a family summit at my place."

Sarah knew that something terrible had happened. The only reason a family summit could be called was for a true emergency of the worst kind. The family knew that they had to drop whatever they were doing and reach the summit within 48 hours; no questions asked.

The following morning her parents and sister flew into SeaTac Airport and were met by Peter and Sarah. The entire family traveled to the Stuart Mansion as a united front, ready to face whatever Aimee had to tell them.

Aimee was in the front rose garden dead heading the blooms when everyone arrived.

"Have you considered pulling out the two bushes in the center and replanting new ones?" Pat inquired.

"Never!" Aimee exclaimed. "Martin planted those and true, they've never bloomed, but they are healthy plants and deserve the right to live and grow."

Aimee hugged her family and then they went inside and gathered around her in the living room to hear her news.

"Several weeks ago I went to the doctor because I have an odd growth on my leg. I thought it was a mole, but it was growing really fast. Yesterday when I went back for the results, I was told I have cancer," Aimee said.

"So, are they going to operate to remove it?" Aimee's mother asked as she took her daughter's hand in hers.

"No, Mom, there is absolutely nothing they can do. I have nodular melanoma and this form of cancer is so aggressive that it has already attached itself to my vital organs. At this rate of progression, the doctor said I have 6 weeks or less before it kills me. He actually said he'd never seen one spread as fast as mine."

No one spoke. Aimee's mother squeezed her hand even tighter while her father hugged her. Aimee burst into tears.

"There has to be something that can be done, Aimee; people survive cancer all the time," Pat said between her tears.

"Not with this type of cancer. It develops vertically and is invasive in depth. I guess it is extremely rare," Aimee replied.

"So, you are just giving up?" Sarah blurted out. "That's not like you, Aimee!"

"No, I'm not giving up; I'm accepting the facts and moving forward. That is why I called everyone here, to discuss Lily," Aimee replied.

Aimee presented her wishes to her family. Since Sarah and Peter were Lily's Godparents, she wanted them to raise her, but not in their apartment in Seattle. She would leave the house in a trust for Lily and they were to raise her in her own home. Lastly, Aimee stated that she would remain in the house until she died, and would arrange for Hospice to take care of her so her family would have some relief during the final days.

The room was silent. No one knew what to say or really what to think. It was Lily's voice that broke the silence. "Mommy told you, didn't she?"

"Yes, sweetheart, Mommy told us," Sarah said as she knelt down to hug her.

"You told her? She's only three!" Pat said in disbelief.

"Yes, I told her. I'm her mother and I wanted to be the one to explain everything to her."

"It will be okay, Aunt Pat," Lily said as she walked over and sat on her mother's lap. "Mommy will be with Daddy, and they can both take care of me, along with Aunt Sarah and Uncle Peter."

"No, honey, you mean Mommy and Daddy will watch over you from heaven," Pat replied.

"No, Aunt Pat, they will live in this house with me and Aunt Sarah and Uncle Peter," she replied as a matter of fact.

"Aimee!" Pat blurted, "You are not condoning that line of thought, are you?"

Giving her daughter a big hug, Aimee said, "Why don't you run up to the nursery and get everything ready for our tea party. I'll be right up and then we can heat up the magic oven and bake a cake to go with the tea."

"Okay, Mommy," she replied and she skipped out of the room and up the stairs. "Don't take too long or your tea will get cold."

"Please tell me you are not encouraging her to believe you and her father will be ghosts, trapped in this house forever," Pat stated.

"Pat," Sarah jumped in, "leave her be. Lily is too young to comprehend the truth about death; if it helps ease her into the reality of losing her mother, then I say let her believe that."

"Well, it's a good thing you didn't leave her with Jeff and me, because I would never agree to encourage a child to believe in ghosts," Pat said.

"Yes, it's a very good thing," Sarah remarked sarcastically.

"So you believe there are ghosts in this house? I'm not surprised, with its gruesome history," Pat responded. "And yes, I did some investigation into your house when we got home after Christmas, and I definitely would not raise my children here."

"Pat, Sarah," Aimee said, "please don't fight over this. The house is not haunted Pat, and it's normal for small children to have imaginary or invisible friends. If my daughter feels comforted thinking her father and I are with her, well, I'm okay with that."

****

Aimee's health deteriorated quickly over the next two weeks and a full-time nursing staff was brought in to care for her around the clock. Her parents arrived from Boise and joined Sarah and Peter, who were already there staying in one of the guest bedrooms so they could look after Lily. By the end of the fourth week, the doctors recommended that anyone who wanted to say good-bye should get there quickly, because the cancer was spreading at an alarming rate.

As she drifted in and out of the morphine-induced sleep, Aimee could hear Lily chatting to her. With all her strength, Aimee fought the drugs to find her way back to consciousness so she could speak with Lily one last time.

"Hey, baby, how are you?" she whispered with a dry, scratchy voice.

"Oh Mommy, you're awake! I'm okay, Daddy has been keeping me company," she said as her Aunt Sarah broke in.

Aimee's eyes quickly shot in Sarah's direction. "Don't worry," Sarah said, placing her hand on Aimee's arm. "It's like you said earlier, having an imaginary friend is cathartic for her at this point."

"He's real, Mommy. I promise I'm not lying."

"Sarah, could you give me a moment with Lily?"

"Sure, I'll go make some tea."

"Mommy, honestly, I'm not telling stories. Daddy comes to visit and he reads me books and he tells me funny stories and he talks funny."

"Oh, he uses funny cartoon voices?"

"No, he just doesn't sound like you and me. He told me he was from Scotland."

"How do you know he's your Daddy?"

"I saw him in a picture with you. He told me where you hid them in your top drawer." Pausing, Lily looked at her mother with tears in her eyes. "You're not mad at me for getting into your things are you?"

"No Luv, I could never be mad with you. Can you tell me what your Daddy wears when he visits you?"

"Oh, that's easy, Mommy. He always wears the same thing. He has blue pants like Uncle Peter wears, a white top and brown shoes."

Lily, is your Daddy here now?"

Looking around the room, Lily replied, "No Mommy. How come you can't see him?'

"I don't know, I used to see him, but then one day he was just gone. How long has he been visiting you?"

"Oh, ever since I was little and afraid of the thunder storms; he would stay with me so I wasn't scared. Do you want me to tell him to visit you?"

"Yes, Honey. Tell your Daddy I need him to visit with me and Aunt Sarah. Tell him it's very urgent."

"Okay, Mommy, I'll be right back," she said as she ran out the door of the bedroom, nearly tripping over Sarah as she entered the room.

"Whoa, slow down Lily or you will hurt yourself."

"Sorry, but Mommy needs me to get Daddy right away."

"Aimee, you shouldn't encourage her like that. What will happen when she realizes you cannot see her dad when she returns with him?" Sarah asked.

"Sarah, it is Martin. I'm too tired to explain everything to you, but I need you to believe her. Tell Lily to show you where I keep the pictures; there's a key in there and it goes to the box locked inside the secret room. You'll find all the answers in there."

"What secret room are you talking about, Aimee?" Sarah asked, thinking her sister was confused from the medications.

"In the nursery, just press the third thistle down on the right side mantel and the door will open."

When Lily returned to the bedroom, her smile was gone and in its place were tiny quivering lips and tears building in her bright blue eyes. "Aunt Sarah, I couldn't find Daddy, I don't know where he is," she said.

"It's alright, sweetheart, she needs to sleep right now," Sarah said as she gave her a big hug and wiped away her tears. "Mommy wants you to show me where the pictures are hidden in her dresser."

Eagerly, Lily ran over to the dresser and pushed back her mother's clothes to reveal a stack of photos and a key with a very old black ribbon tied around it.

"Thank you, sweetheart," Sarah said. "I need to do something for your mommy, so I'd like you to go down and spend time with your grandparents. Tell Uncle Peter to meet me in the nursery; it's very important."

"Okay, but when Mommy wakes up, you come and get me, so I can get Daddy for her."

"I promise Lily, I'll get you the minute she wakes," Sarah said as she kissed the top of her head and sent her on her way downstairs.

Sarah summoned a nurse to sit with Aimee while she went upstairs to the nursery. Following her sister's instructions, she pressed the third thistle and waited for the panel to open and then she entered the secret room and located the locked box. Sarah brought the box out of the room and sat down on the nursery floor to unlock it and look at the contents. At first she did not know what to make of the old book, a bag full of herbs, the locket she had seen Aimee wearing the night of the street dance, a bag with ten very old gold coins and an antique dagger. What was Aimee involved in? Opening the book to the page bookmarked by a white ribbon, she found the letters written by Eliza. Sarah read through everything and, knowing the history of the house, found it plausible.

The last letter Sarah opened was actually written by Aimee. It recounted the entire period from when she first met Martin in her bedroom, up to the point where he vanished after the third full moon. The last paragraph of the letter read:

Sarah, I can only trust you and Peter with the most precious thing that Martin and I have, our daughter. Please trust in her because she is a very special child. Use your best judgment to know when it is the right time to share the contents of this box with her. I do not know what happens after we die, but if possible, I will find Martin on the other side, and together we will quietly watch over our child.

Tears were streaming down Sarah's face when Peter entered the room. Sitting down on the floor next to his wife, he held her close and listened as she told him what Aimee had said earlier and what she found in the box. Sarah was not surprised when Peter said he believed her and asked to have a few minutes to look through the items before they placed them back into the box. Peter suggested keeping out one picture for Lily; it was of Aimee and Martin, and Peter planned to frame it and place it on Lily's bedside table.

When Sarah returned to Aimee's bedroom, the nurse was on her way to the kitchen for fresh water. As Sarah opened the door she discovered Martin was sitting on the bed next to Aimee, holding her hand.

"Hello Martin," Sarah said as she closed and locked the bedroom door. "I don't want anyone walking in while I'm talking to you, just in case they can't see you."

"Good idea," Martin said. "Right now only you, Aimee and Lily can see me."

"I just finished reading the documents Aimee stored away. It explained everything about you and the house," she said, wiping the tears from her face.

"She loved, you Martin. Well, actually she still loves you. The only thing that kept her from losing her mind after you died, or vanished, well whatever happened, was Lily."

"I wanted to show myself when she came home that day, running through the house telling me she was pregnant and that we were going to be parents."

"That sounds like Aimee," Sarah said with a laugh. "So why didn't you?"

"I thought it best if she believed I had crossed over. I did not want her sitting in this house, alone, for the rest of her life just waiting to die so we could be together. I wanted her to live and find love and happiness."

"That was very noble of you, Martin," Sarah said, "it just didn't work. She loves you too much to let you go. I actually think she can feel your presence in the house, that's why she wants to die here, so you will be there to greet her when she passes away."

Aimee thought she was dreaming and that the combination of drugs was making her think she could hear Martin. Opening her eyes, Aimee asked, "Sarah, who are you talking to?"

"Aimee, I'm talking to Martin. He's on the bed next to you."

With great effort Aimee turned her head, pulling the leads and tubes with it, and looked up at Martin and tried to smile. He was just as beautiful as she remembered him; her heart jumped with joy to see him again.

Martin reached down and took her hand in his.

"Am I dead?" she asked. "I can feel you touching me."

"No, my love, but you have begun to cross over and I will stay right here until it's over."

"I thought I'd lost you, Martin," Aimee said with tears pooling in her eyes.

"I told you once before that you couldn't lose me, because I will be with you forever."

Sarah quietly walked over to the door and unlocked it. "I'll give you two a few minutes and then I'll send Lily up," she said, opening the door and leaving the room.

"I think we misunderstood Eliza's warning," Aimee said.

"Yes, I agree. She didn't mean I would die if we used the dark art spell, she meant you would. If I knew this was the consequence of what we were about to do, I would never have allowed you to go through with it."

"You had to, Martin; it was the only way for you to live on. Actually, we will both live on, through Lily. I regret nothing," she said, trying to squeeze his hand, but found she was too weak to do so.

"Neither do I," Martin said as he leaned over and kissed her on the forehead.

As each family member went in and said their last goodbye to Aimee, Sarah pulled Peter aside and told him not to acknowledge seeing Martin when he walked into the room, as they were the only ones besides Aimee and Lily that could see him.

When Pat emerged from the room, she realized Lily was standing next to Sarah with a beaming smile on her face. "Lily, don't you understand this is a very sad moment and not a time to be laughing?"

"I'm not laughing, Aunt Pat."

"Then why are you standing there with a big smile on your face? Your mother is dying!"

"Because Daddy is in there holding Mommy's hand and she's happy that he's back."

"Good Lord, do you people see what you are doing to her, letting her believe in such crap? She will be spending the rest of her life in therapy over this!" Pat said as she stormed down the stairs.

Sarah took Lily's hand in hers. "She didn't mean to yell at you sweetie, she's just very upset that her baby sister is dying. You go ahead and smile as big as you want. It will make your mother happy to see you smiling."

Taking Peter's hand, the three of them entered Aimee's room. Nurse Maria was adjusting the morphine drip and checking the monitor. "Only moments left," she said as she left them alone in the room.

"Your Daddy and I love you very much, Lily," Aimee said.

"I know Mommy, and I love both of you."

"Promise us you will let Aunt Sarah and Uncle Peter love you, as much as we do," Aimee said.

Running over to the bed and hugging her mom as best she could, Lily said, "I will Mommy. I will be a very good girl for them, just like I am for you."

Aimee placed her hand on Lily's head one last time. For a brief moment she could feel the soft curls of her daughter's strawberry blonde hair and then she felt nothing. The alarm on the heart monitor sounded, and the nurse rushed in to turn it off and then quickly left the room.

Martin got up from the bed and extended his hands out towards Aimee. Within a few seconds, her spirit rose from her body and she placed her hands in his while he helped her stand beside him. Martin pulled her close and kissed her long and hard. "I will love you for eternity," he said.

Aimee looked over to Sarah and Peter, who were comforting each other. Lily was still standing by the bed, but her sorrow had again turned into a beaming smile.

"Oh Mommy, you look beautiful again," she said.

"We will love you forever, Lily," she said, blowing her a kiss.

Turning away from the bed where her body remained, Martin and Aimee took a few steps forward and vanished.

A few days later, a private ceremony was held in the Stuart cemetery. The only participants were Sarah, Peter and Lily. Aimee's final wish was to have her ashes buried in the same grave as Martin's bones. She wanted to lay with him for all of eternity. Peter carefully dug a small hole in the center of the flower bed, which

Aimee had planted above Martin's grave, then Lily placed the box containing her mother's ashes into the hole.

The next morning the family woke to a surprise. The two white rose bushes Martin had planted in the center of the front circular drive were now in full majestic bloom.

www.ingramcontent.com/pod-product-compliance
Lightning Source LLC
Chambersburg PA
CBHW060810120626
46557CB00001B/154